Tales of a Wandering Warthog

I ran between the robber's legs, causing him to fall (p. 25).

Tales of a Wandering Warthog

Tom Sinclair
Illustrated by John C. Wallner

Albert Whitman & Company
Niles, Illinois

This book is dedicated
with love to
Cynthia Bryant
for believing, and to
Emery Bryson,
Tom Soter &
Allan Wilder
—fine fellows all.

Library of Congress Cataloging in Publication Data

Sinclair, Tom.
    Tales of a wandering warthog.

    Summary: A talking warthog and his teenage human
friends outwit evildoers in exotic settings in outer
space and on earth.
    1. Children's stories, American. [1. Science
fiction]   I. Wallner, John C., ill. II. Title.
PZ7.S6119Tal   1985   [Fic]   84-19621
ISBN 0-8075-7754-5

The text of this book is printed in twelve-point Baskerville

Text © 1985 by Tom Sinclair
Illustrations © 1985 by John C. Wallner
Published in 1985 by Albert Whitman & Company, Niles, Illinois
Published simultaneously in Canada by General Publishing, Limited, Toronto
Printed in U.S.A. All rights reserved.

10   9   8   7   6   5   4   3   2   1

Contents

Prologue

In a red-brick cottage by a bubbling lake, the most intelligent warthog on Earth squatted comfortably on a brown leather chair, surveying a massive volume that lay on the desk before him. The Warthog, who was wearing a specially designed red silk smoking jacket, squinted at the book through the lenses of his golden pince-nez. Its title, *Tales of a Wandering Warthog,* looked up at him in bold, gold-embossed lettering. Those who knew him would have been able to detect pride shining through the narrowed eyes in the crinkled brown face. Pride, and something more; a certain wistfulness that was not quite sorrow was carved on the noble features as he sat there in his study, a warm fire burning in the hearth to his right.

There was a hesitant knock at the study door. The Warthog slowly turned his head in the direction of the sound. "Come in, Irene," he called.

The door opened and in walked Irene Springer, the Warthog's faithful housekeeper and companion. She carried a tray which held a large wooden bowl of shredded lettuce and sliced tomatoes and a tall glass of iced ginger ale with a long straw.

"Suppertime, Mr. Warthog," said the girl as she set the tray down on his desk.

"Thank you, Irene," said the Warthog. "You are most kind. I've no idea how I would get along without you."

The girl smiled. Then, as her eyes dropped to the book on the desk, the smile faded and was replaced by a serious expression. She had half turned to go when, with a look of determined resolution, she pivoted to address her employer.

"Mr. Warthog," said Irene Springer, her pretty eyes flashing, "I have been patient with you. In all the time you have spent writing your book, I have not asked to look at it. Nor have I bothered you—I realize that a writer needs a certain amount of solitude. But now the book has been published, and you have not even invited me to look at it, much less given me a copy to read. I am really quite beside myself! After all this time, I know precious little about your past life. I ask you, sir: is this any way to repay me for my faithful service?"

The Warthog's face wore an expression of dismay and embarrassment. "Sweet Irene," he said earnestly, "please forgive my thoughtlessness. I have no excuse. To be sure, I have been wrapped up in my project these past months. But I always intended to give you the first copy of my *Tales*. Of course, you may have this copy on the desk for your own." The Warthog hesitated, pondering. "I don't know how to make this up to you, Irene.

8

Perhaps, if you would have the patience, as soon as I have finished this delicious meal, you would allow me to tell you the first portion of my life story in detail."

Irene Springer smiled with delight. "Eat up then, Mr. Warthog," she said, sitting in a reclining chair to the Warthog's left. "I have waited a long time to learn your story, and a few minutes more will do no harm." As the Warthog began to eat his supper, Irene crossed her legs and waited for him to start his narrative.

(Editor's note: The text that follows is the story the Warthog related to Irene Springer.)

1
Off to America

I was born in the African bush on a hot August morning in the
year 1952, the only child of two elderly warthogs of the species
Phacochoerus africanus. My mother tells me that just seconds after
my birth, I greeted her with a hearty "Good morning, Mother!"
I do not remember this, but I know that I was born with a full
knowledge not only of English but also of several other languages,
as well as the somewhat primitive grunting tongue used by warthogs and other beasts of the bush.

My parents were amazed and pleased to have a son who could
speak at so young an age. Because they had once been kept as
pets by a kindly missionary, they were able to speak several African dialects and somewhat broken English. They kept this a
secret from the other warthogs except Old Zareemba, our chief
and wisest member. My parents and Old Zareemba warned me
that speaking in a human tongue among my own kind would

cause jealousy. Old Zareemba said there had only been one other beast in our tribe who was gifted with human speech. Envious warthogs had driven him away, and he was never heard from again.

No one found out my secret, but my early years were still unhappy. I was smaller than the other boys and considered the runt of the tribe. And I was always afraid that I would somehow slip and reveal my ability to talk.

My sleeping habits also differed from those of my fellow warthogs. I preferred to retire in the evenings and be up and about early in the day. The rest of the tribe were nocturnal. This was all right with me, for considering how I was treated, the less time I was forced to spend with them, the better I liked it.

Because of my size, I was left out of games, and the other boys played tricks on me. On one occasion, they organized a race and invited me to join in. They said they would give me a head start because I was so small. I ran as fast as I could, only to find that the others had never followed. When I returned to them, hot and ashamed, they jeered and laughed.

After that, I stayed away from them. Still, they found ways to trick me. When we all grew tusks, they considered it great fun to sharpen theirs on my hide while I was asleep or eating.

As was our custom, I was allowed to choose my own name when I was one year old. Until then I had been addressed as "Little Silence," for I kept to myself. I chose "Red," my favorite color. So I was called for about a week until Horgor, a fat, mean warthog who had never liked me, gouged me in the side with his tusk. As I began to bleed, he laughingly called to a group of friends, "Red can now see red!" This hurt my feelings more than my hide, and as I turned away from the group I vowed that I would remain nameless for life.

My parents knew that I was suffering, but there was little they could do to make life easier for me. To escape bullies like Horgor, I would sometimes leave the tribe for days at a time. I wandered for miles in the African grasslands. I knew there must be some-place where I could live happily, but where?

One day I found a man-made cabin deep in the jungle. It was deserted. Inside I found shelves of books. (My father had told me about reading, though he himself could not do it.) I knocked a volume from a shelf and pawed it open with my hoof. Imagine my surprise when I found I could understand the words! The book was *David Copperfield* by Charles Dickens, and I spent the entire day reading it. I had seen men before, at a seaport I some-times observed, but reading about them made me certain that my destiny was in the world of human beings. David Copperfield's hardships and hopes reminded me of my own. It was only when the sun went down that I closed the book, to return to it the next day.

In the next few years, I visited that cabin until I had read every book inside. Each one made me hunger more to be a part of the society of men and women. I would watch them with fascination from the bushes that fringed the seaport. Most wart-hogs try to avoid humans, but I ached to speak with them, to pour out the secrets in my heart.

Though I shunned and feared most of my kind, I was blessed with one friend. He was a warthog of my own age named Jack

Ham. Sometimes Jack came along on my forays to the seaport, and I would tell him my feelings. I confessed to him that I felt an outcast among my own kind. Jack would listen patiently as I grunted to him in Warthog, but I could sense he did not fully understand all I told him. Still, it was a great comfort to have one friend to talk to.

When I was fully grown, I was less than two-thirds the size of a normal warthog. Not only did the boys mock me, but the females also treated me with scorn. Yet I developed a crush on one who seemed kinder than the others. Her name was Jasmeena, and she was Jack's sister.

One day I asked her to walk with me through the jungle. I told her I knew of a secluded spot with many puddles where we could wallow. When she accepted, I felt as if I were on a pink cloud of joy. We agreed to go early the next evening, when the moon would be full.

We met beneath a tree in a clearing. I had sharpened my tusks and shined my hooves for our date. Jasmeena looked so lovely in the moonlight that tears came into my eyes. (I can almost see her dainty hooves and tiny tusks before me now!) Beside her I felt almost large and strong.

We strolled off toward the mud puddles together, talking easily. My worries seemed a thing of the past. Then Horgor stepped out of the jungle in front of us.

"What's this?" he cried. "The little runt out with the prettiest sow in the tribe! What a waste! Jasmeena, let Horgor show you a good time!"

Full of anger and fear, I attacked him blindly. We fought, and

Tales of a Wandering Warthog 13

he beat me badly. Jasmeena went off with him, leaving me bleeding on the ground.

My shame and sorrow had never seemed so complete. This incident made me realize that I must leave the tribe for good. The next day I told my parents that I had decided to go away and seek my fortune among men. My mother cried but respected my decision. My father told me I should speak to Old Zareemba before going, and I went to seek him out.

Old Zareemba looked at me for some time after I told him my plans. When he spoke I had to listen carefully, for his grunts were very quiet.

"I have watched you, young Warthog," he began. "I have seen you suffer because you are not like the others. But you do not yet see how wonderful it is to be different! Those who torment you are very ordinary. They will never have the opportunity to learn what you will."

I looked at him in puzzlement. It did not seem to me good to be different; it had only brought me pain. I told him this.

"Ah!" he smiled. "But through pain there is growth. But I can see that you do not understand yet. I will tell you, though, that your decision is the right one. I will also tell you that this village has not seen the last of you. I think when we see you again it will be in quite a different light. Good luck to you!"

I asked Old Zareemba just what he meant by all of this, but he only smiled, refusing to say more. I left him, confused and unhappy.

That was on a September morning in 1965. I set off through the jungle toward the seaport I had observed so often. Timid as

14

I was, I planned to sail to some foreign place. I thought nothing could be lonelier than the life I led now. Although I regretted leaving my parents, Jack Ham, and Old Zareemba, I cared for no one else. The joy and excitement I felt told me I was taking the correct action.

There was much confusion when I arrived at the harbor. Most people I met seemed to be as frightened of me as I was of them. I said hello, very meekly, to an elderly woman, and she fainted dead away. I finally summoned up enough courage to speak to a baggage boy who was only too delighted to meet a talking warthog. He listened with great interest when I told him my plans.

"So, you want to take a ship to a foreign place, Mr. Warthog?" said the youth. "Well, now, we've a rule that says no stray animals on shipboard. And you say you've no money? I really don't know if I can help you out."

We stood looking at each other for several moments. My face must have betrayed my disappointment. I was about to go when the boy's grim expression suddenly brightened.

"Just a second there, Warthog," he said. "I've an idea! Wait right here!" He soon returned, smiling widely, with two teenaged boys following him.

"Mr. Warthog," he announced, "here are Troy and Adam Armstrong, two American brothers who have been on vacation. They are leaving on the next boat to New York City. They've agreed that you may travel as their pet. I hope you won't mind sleeping in the baggage compartment, but it was the only arrangement I could make."

I assured him that any arrangement was fine with me and

expressed my gratitude. He cut me short with a wave of his hand and wished me good luck, saying he was very busy. He left the three of us standing awkwardly on the dock.

"You really *can* talk," said one of the boys at length, looking at me with undisguised amazement. "I thought that guy was putting us on!" He was an eager-looking boy with large gray eyes and long, curly brown hair.

"Most certainly," I said, grinning.

"Absolutely astounding!" said the other boy. He resembled his brother greatly, except that his hair was blonde and short.

I examined the two as they stood in front of me. Adam, the long-haired one, was wearing a sloppy outfit. (I later learned his clothes were blue jeans and a T-shirt.) Troy presented a more serious front to the world. He was dressed in neat gray slacks and a white button-down shirt. I liked the boys instantly. As we stood there, I had a feeling that our meeting was to be one of the most significant events of my life.

We had several hours to wait before the ship sailed, so the boys took me to a nearby restaurant to get better acquainted. I turned quite a few heads when I walked in and squatted at a table atop a chair, but Troy and Adam acted so natural that I soon stopped feeling conspicuous. They ordered a bowl of ginger ale for me (to this day I remain exceedingly fond of that drink), and I gave them a brief history of my life. They were fascinated by the fact that I had been born knowing how to speak, and they agreed that I had been wise to leave the bush.

I urged them to tell me about themselves. Orphaned early (their parents were geologists who had died in a plane crash),

16

they had been brought up by their elderly Aunt Aramantha in New York City. Troy, the blonde brother, was a top student who excelled in chemistry, rocketry, and biology. It was through a summer scholarship he had won that he and Adam had come to study African wildlife. Wild-haired Adam, at fifteen a year younger than Troy, was an average student who hoped to be a writer someday. He had a ready smile and a quick sense of humor. By the time the ship's whistle blew, I felt I had known Adam and Troy for years.

We set out for sea that afternoon. I did not mind being boxed in the baggage compartment because the boys spent their free moments with me. At night they took me for walks along the lower deck. I told them about the books I had read in the cabin, most of which were by British authors. I was curious to know if New York was like the places described by Dickens and Sir Arthur Conan Doyle. They laughed at this and said things had changed quite a bit over a century. They described buildings that rose higher than one hundred men would stand if they were placed one atop the other. Also, they said, there were machines which flew through the air, much faster than any boat. All this was astonishing to me.

The boys brought me bread, vegetables, and ginger ale and something even more nourishing—their friendship. Some days Adam would sit with me and write poetry, or Troy would bring the blueprints for some new device he was working on. Adam told me in confidence that Dr. Fredericks, Troy's science teacher and a rocket expert, considered him to be a genius. The teacher trusted Troy enough to involve him in some very sophisticated secret projects, including work with the U.S. government. One had something to do with space travel.

The days passed quickly, and by the time we reached America I had made two solid friends. My biggest worry was that soon I would lose them.

The night before we docked, I couldn't sleep. My little crate had never seemed so cramped. What lay ahead for me? I felt as if I had used all my courage to board the ship and had none left to face my new life. What if I had to leave the boys and make my own way in a strange land?

Early the next morning, Troy and Adam came to see me. They looked worried, and I asked what was wrong.

"Mr. Warthog," began Troy, slowly, "I guess you know that we've both grown very fond of you."

"As I have of you," I said.

"It's like this," continued Troy. "We'd really like for you to stay on with us, at least for a while. The problem is our Aunt Aramantha. She doesn't like animals, and I doubt she would let us keep a warthog."

My heart sank at these words. Visions of wandering alone and friendless in a strange country sprang into my head. To lose these two friends after so many years of loneliness and sorrow seemed too great a blow!

The three of us regarded each other during an uneasy silence. Suddenly, Adam banged his fist against the wall.

"Aunt Aramantha can go fly a kite!" he said. "I say we keep the Warthog in our room without telling her. It won't be hard to rig up some kind of quarters for him, and Auntie doesn't notice

18

much, anyway. I've grown too fond of this little fellow to abandon him now!"

Troy looked undecided. He turned away from the intensity of his brother's gaze, and his eyes met mine. He looked at me for just a second, then grinned.

"All right, then," said Troy. "You've got a home with us!"

Soon, crouched inside a small wooden crate with airholes in the sides, I found myself with Troy, Adam, and Aunt Aramantha (who had met the boys at the pier) in a taxicab headed for the East Side of Manhattan. During the ride I peeked out one of the airholes for a look at Aunt Aramantha. She was a pleasant-looking, plump woman with silver hair and rimless spectacles. She chattered along, then suddenly asked Adam what was in the wooden crate on his lap.

"Oh, this," began Adam, flustered. "Why this is . . . er . . ."

Just then the cab stopped short, throwing everyone forward. After the confusion was settled, Troy made a comment about New York cab drivers, and he and Adam laughed noisily. Aunt Aramantha was visibly shaken and asked no more questions about the crate in which I crouched.

Shortly after, we arrived at the Armstrong apartment. Adam pried open the lid to my box, and I leapt out onto a wooden floor. I saw a big room with bright yellow walls and a bed, bookshelf, and desk for each boy. In the center wall was a closet. Adam opened it and turned on a light.

"I think, Mr. Warthog, that once we clear out some of the junk, this will make a wonderful bedroom for you. Take a look."

I peered into the closet and saw it was quite deep. Adam was already taking shoes, papers, and scientific models off the floor.

"What do you think?" he asked when he had finished.

"I'd say it looks like home," I answered, feeling a glow of warmth at the kindness of these two humans toward one so different. As I stood looking into the closet, there was a sharp rap at the bedroom door.

"It's Aunt Aramantha!" whispered Troy hoarsely. "Quick, get into the closet!"

I bolted into the closet, and Adam slammed the door on me. A second later I heard the outside door open.

"Supper in half an hour, boys," she said.

"Okay, Aunt Aramantha," chimed Troy and Adam.

There was silence for a moment, and then Adam opened the door. I peered tensely up at him.

"That was a close shave," Troy breathed.

"That's for sure," laughed Adam. "Any closer and we'd have lost a layer of skin!" All three of us laughed nervously.

In the weeks that followed, things worked out nicely. I felt more at home with the boys than I had ever felt in the bush. I slept comfortably on a bed Troy made for me by folding up a sleeping bag. Adam took to calling me "Wart" for short. Troy had wanted to call me "P.A." (short for *Phacochoerus africanus*, my scientific name). Though I did not want any official name, "Mr. Warthog" was too formal, and "P.A." was, in Adam's words, "egghead hogwash." So the name Wart stuck.

The brothers took me around the city, and I was quite impressed with New York. At first the hurrying people, the cars, and the noise frightened me, but after a few outings I came to feel a part of it all. Many New Yorkers were quite interested in me; wherever we went, people would stop and stare. For a while this made me self-conscious, but soon I came to enjoy the attention. I was no longer the shy, inexperienced warthog I had been just weeks ago.

Adam brought me to a tailor friend. A splendid fellow named Richard, he took my measurements and designed a number of outfits. It took a while to grow accustomed to wearing clothes, but after a bit I could not imagine leaving home undressed. Richard made me several warthog-sized suits as well as sweaters, pajamas, blue jeans, and an outfit of red-striped shorts with a matching shirt. I had everything a young warthog could ask for.

During the day, when the boys were at school, I had pretty much the run of the apartment. Since Aunt Aramantha was often out, shopping or having lunch with friends, I spent much time in her well-stocked library. She had many books by my old favorites, Dickens and Doyle. The boys also gave me some of their most well-loved books. Adam introduced me to the James Bond series by Ian Fleming and to Raymond Chandler's private eye, Phillip Marlowe. Troy was a big science-fiction fan and recommended books by Robert A. Heinlein, Theodore Sturgeon, and Frank Herbert. All of these I enjoyed greatly.

A couple of times, Aunt Aramantha came upon me reading in the library. Fortunately, she was not wearing her glasses. Troy had told me she couldn't make out very much without them, and he was right. Once she set a cup of tea down on my back, apparently thinking that I was a coffee table!

Living there with the boys, I began to feel much better about myself. There were times when I thought about my unhappy years in the bush, but these memories grew less painful as time passed. Still, I was very different from human beings, and I could not help wondering where my true place in life was.

Each night, after Troy and Adam ate their dinner, they would bring me mine, mostly vegetables and fruit and always ginger ale. (Troy laughed when he told me that Aunt Aramantha was pleased that the boys were now eating plenty of vegetables!) While the boys did their homework, I would sit quietly on the floor, reading from one of the textbooks they were not using. I picked up a basic knowledge of world history, politics, and mathematics (that gave me the hardest time!) in this way.

The boys argued over what radio station to listen to; Adam liked rock 'n' roll, while Troy preferred classical or jazz. I wound up as their mediator; we all agreed that each brother could hear the music of his choice on alternate nights. This was good for me because I was interested in hearing all these types of music.

Some evenings we would watch "the tube," as Adam called it. Of course, television was quite new to me and something of a marvel. The boys and I particularly enjoyed "The Man from U.N.C.L.E." and "Bonanza."

Adam and I went down to Greenwich Village several times to hear live music. We heard the Blues Project, the Lovin' Spoonful, and even Bob Dylan, who had just begun to play electric music. Adam also liked a number of British bands. I remember him saying he would give his eyeteeth to be able to see the Yardbirds or the Rolling Stones in a live performance. He often carried a harmonica, which he would play when the mood struck him.

22

Troy, for his part, frequently stayed up long after Adam and I went to sleep. He was working on some scientific project about which he said very little.

The days passed in this manner until a couple of days before Christmas, when the boys awakened me from a nap in the early afternoon. Each had a large bag on his shoulders, and they were smiling broadly.

"We're going to give you your Christmas present a little early, Wart," said Troy.

"What's in those bags?" I asked, still drowsy.

"Follow us, and you'll see," said Adam.

The boys led me to the bathroom where they opened up the bags and dumped the contents into the tub. It was dirt! Troy turned on the water and began mixing the dirt and water with a large spoon, whistling as he did so.

"I remember your saying that you missed your mud baths since coming to America," said Adam. It was true. I had told him that a couple of weeks ago.

"Fellows, I don't know what to say," I said. Peering over the tub's edge, I saw that the mud was of a dark brown color. It smelled rich, earthy, and delightful.

"Don't say anything," said Troy, turning off the water. "Just enjoy." With those words he and Adam picked me up bodily and dumped me into the tub. I spent the rest of the afternoon wallowing in pleasure.

After the mud bath, I took a regular bath with soap and water. I had come to value cleanliness since coming to America. I felt bad about having no money to buy the boys anything for Christmas, but I promised myself that the following year I would some-how get them presents.

About four days after the holiday, Troy woke us up very early and announced that he had a surprise. He looked very pleased. "Dr. Fredericks does work for the government," Troy said. "I have been helping him with a top-secret rocket project for some time now. He has given me three priority passes to see the ship launched today! It's piloted by a trained monkey and powered by a lot of computers and radar. Its destination is the red planet: Mars!"

"Gosh-a-roony!" exclaimed Adam with sleepy sarcasm.

"I knew you'd be excited," said Troy with a satisfied grin. "We must leave soon. The secret launching pad is in the wilds of Staten Island, so we'll need a couple of hours traveling time. Now, don't mention this to anyone!"

We dressed hurriedly and caught the subway downtown to the famed Staten Island Ferry. By this time I was an old hand at riding the subways, and I felt like a native New Yorker. As usual, I attracted a lot of staring and gaping from people on the train. My smile and cheerful "Good day" produced a number of varied reactions, most often a mumbled "Hello" back and a quick look in the opposite direction. I must admit I found all this fun.

It was at the Fourteenth Street stop that a shifty-looking young man got on our car. He had oily black hair and quick, darting eyes, and he wore a long, dirty raincoat. Our car was fairly crowded. I watched the fellow as he maneuvered himself next to a pretty blonde girl and dipped his hand into her purse, removing a wallet. No one else seemed to have noticed.

24

At the next stop he started to get off, but I ran between his legs, causing him to fall. He dropped the girl's wallet.

"Pardon me," I said, "but I don't think that this belongs to you." I picked the wallet up in my teeth and returned it to the girl. The fellow in the raincoat fled in a wild-eyed frenzy.

The entire car applauded, and Adam and Troy looked at me with pride. I felt a special glow when the girl knelt down and gratefully stroked my head.

It was near noon, the launch time, when we arrived at the site. As we showed our three priority passes, the guard at the gate eyed me with a look I did not like. All along the corridor leading toward the rocket, uniformed guards glared at me suspiciously. I grinned and murmured "Good day" to them, but here I got no response save for cold stares. The guards made me uneasy, and I mentioned it to Troy.

"Oh, they're just doing their jobs, you know," he said. "One can't be too careful on a top-secret rocket base like this. I understand they recently captured a communist spy lurking around in a wolf-man mask!"

We reached the end of the long corridor just then, and I stopped short, amazed. There, supported by scaffolding, was the tall, cylindrical rocket ship we had come to see. Its tip pointed toward a large round hole in the white ceiling. Near the rocket's base a number of officials stood talking. Troy hailed one of them.

"Dr. Fredericks!" he called.

A thin, gray-haired man came over to us. His smile froze when he noticed me.

"Why, Troy—Adam—you are just in time. In less than four

minutes you will witness something amazing. Uh, Troy, this creature here . . ."

"Is a good friend of ours, Dr. Fredericks," piped in Adam quickly. "Allow me to introduce our guest, Mr. Warthog."

As we were speaking, two of the guards (whom I had noticed conferring in whispers a moment before) approached our party. Big, hulking fellows they were, with cruel expressions.

"Hey, you," said one, addressing me. "What are you doing here? And what the blazes are you?"

I felt a lump in my throat and had to struggle to keep my voice from shaking. "I am here as a guest of Troy Armstrong and his brother Adam, in answer to your first question. As to your second: I am a warthog, sir."

The guard who had spoken turned to his companion, and for a few moments they spoke in low tones. I thought I could make out words like "spy" and "mutant commie freak." Troy and Adam heard also, for I saw them exchange worried glances.

Just then all attention was diverted to a ladder at the bottom of the rocket which reached to an open hatchway in the ship's side. A monkey had been led up to it and had begun to climb the ladder.

Their curiosity regarding the monkey satisfied, the guards turned back to me.

"What's your name?" one asked me.

"I have none," I said. I began to explain my decision to remain nameless, when he cut me off.

"A warthog without a name, huh? Might it be Chekhov, or Stavinski, maybe? Haw! You'd better come with us, 'comrade.'"

The guard raised a menacing-looking club over his head, and I did not doubt that he intended to bring it down on my snout. A wave of terror washed over me. I felt the way I had felt in the old days, when I was bullied and attacked in the bush. I snatched a quick look at the corridor through which we had come, but it was blocked off by a throng of uniformed guards. Without thinking, I bolted toward the rocket. Frantically, I scrambled up after the monkey. I was vaguely aware of the sound of agitated voices to my rear. At the same time I heard over a loudspeaker:

"Helena 1, prepare for blast-off. TEN . . . NINE . . ."

I flung myself through the hatchway. Looking down, I saw Adam, followed by Troy, racing up the ladder after me.

"EIGHT . . . SEVEN . . . SIX . . . FIVE . . ."

Adam jumped through the hatchway.

"FOUR . . . THREE . . . TWO . . ."

As the panel of the hatchway began to shut, in leapt Troy. The panel clicked closed, shutting out the last sounds from outside.

"ONE . . . Blast off!"

Before any of us had time to catch our breath, we had lifted off into the unknown!

2

The Purple Planet

The noise and momentum of our takeoff left us all stunned and speechless. Then it hit us: we were actually on board a rocket ship hurtling into space! It was Adam who spoke first.

"Those idiots!" he cried angrily. "It should be those jerks going to their deaths in this thing, not us!"

I felt awful, for I realized that I was the cause of the trouble. Gazing at the floor, I cleared my throat to speak.

"It's my fault," I said. "If I hadn't panicked perhaps we could have reasoned with them and straightened out this mess."

"Don't blame yourself, Wart," said Troy. "It was ignorance and prejudice that put us in this rocket ship. But things aren't as bad as you think. You guys forget that I studied the blueprints for this rocket. I could bring us back to Earth at any time by readjusting the controls. However, I would rather return as one of the first four Earth-beings to land on Mars! What do you say?"

28

Adam and I looked at him, and then at each other, astounded. "What you are proposing, Troy, is fantastic," I said.

"Nuts is more like it," said Adam. "But Troy, assuming you could pull it off, there are a whole bunch of questions we have to look at: How long will this trip take? Can we survive in deep space? What will we eat?"

"By my calculations," began Troy, "we can reach Mars in approximately three weeks. And this ship is equipped with six months' supply of air and artificial gravity, basically duplicating existing conditions on Earth. As far as nourishment, the ship is stocked with hundreds of bananas . . ."

"Bananas!" cried Adam with a pained look on his face.

". . . as well as," continued Troy severely, "thousands of protein pills. When you wash them down with the energy juice that flows from the taps, they expand in your stomach. They make you feel full and give more nutrients than any of us are used to. The monkey here was trained to push buttons and pull levers to set oxygen and gravity distribution functions into operation when he hears the ringing of preset bells. Otherwise, the ship pretty much runs itself. Unless either of you object, Mars, here we come!"

I was quite excited at the thought of being the first warthog on Mars, and I told Troy I was game. Adam grumbled that he had a date to take a girl named Janie to a poetry reading the following Saturday night, but in the end he came around. As for the monkey, he was a likeable little creature whom we decided to call Christopher. Since he could not speak, he offered no objections.

During the next several days, I discovered that life on board a rocket rushing through space was no hardship. Between bananas, protein pills, and the delicious energy juice we drank, I found myself feeling more fit than I had in some time. Troy showed Adam and me the workings of the ship: the computer-run engine, gravity converter, radar energizer, and other contraptions which neither of us could figure out. Fortunately, Troy seemed to understand all that he did on board the ship, and Christopher, for his part, would pull levers and push buttons whenever one of the automatic bells went off.

There was a kind of timeless quality inside that rocket. We had no idea of day or night, so we slept and ate whenever the urge struck us. My only complaint was that there was nothing to read. We had to make up our own entertainment. Adam and I had great fun composing nonsensical poems together; I would toss out a line and he would follow it with one of his own. Then it would be my turn, and so on. It seemed at the time that some of these poems were quite clever, particularly the ones he wrote to Janie. It is possible, though, that—like so many things remembered from youth—they were not really that wonderful.

Adam also provided music with his harmonica. He could blow some very pretty blues. I appreciated this, though Troy would clap his hands over his ears whenever Adam started to play. One evening (though it may well have been high noon back on Earth), when Adam was playing a particularly mournful number, I found tears welling in my eyes. The music had made me melancholy, and I wondered what my fate was to be and why I seemed so different from everyone else. It was a question I often asked myself, and once more I could find no answer. But I promised myself to try to live in the present, and I was grateful that I had the friendship of Adam and Troy.

On what Troy calculated to be our nineteenth day in space, he announced that we were very near Mars. He was peering intently into a viewscreen at the console, muttering to himself.

"How does it look?" I asked, for I saw an uneasy expression come over his face.

"Wart, I've made a mistake. Like a fool I didn't allow for the extra weight of the three of us, and I now see that we are slightly off course."

" 'Slightly off course'?" said Adam, raising one eyebrow. "Is that something like being 'slightly doomed'?"

"Let me worry about that," said Troy, scowling at his brother. He bent over to adjust the Emergency Control Board, which was directly beneath the console. After a few frantic maneuvers, he leaned back, smiling smugly. "In fifteen minutes we will be landing on Phobos, the nearer of Mars's two moons. And there are breathable air, gravity, and all sorts of life on its surface, according to the scanner!"

"Great!" shouted Adam in relief.

Those next fifteen minutes were the longest in my life. The tension built as we watched Troy manipulate the controls. At last he announced we would land in thirty seconds. I closed my eyes and listened to the blood pounding in my head as I counted to thirty. I opened my eyes when there was a slight bump, and I found that Troy had brought us to a smooth landing on the surface of Phobos. The three of us let out a huge cheer, accompanied by Christopher's excited chattering. I wondered nervously who or what we would find on Phobos.

Troy pushed the hatch button, and we stepped forward to get our first view of Phobos.

The four of us stood at the portal, gazing out upon a singularly beautiful planet. In front of us stretched a field filled with lavender vegetation. The air smelled sweet and was quite breathable, confirming Troy's report, and all around us were sounds of animal life. The temperature was a pleasant seventy-five degrees.

Christopher scampered down the ladder onto the planet's surface, where he began chasing a creature that looked something like a butterfly with purplish-tinted wings. The rest of us followed, and I felt a thrill as I planted my hooves on the strange lavender grass.

"It's beautiful," said Adam.

"And we are the first earthlings ever to see this place," said Troy in wonderment.

"I wonder if there are any girls," said Adam.

"Look," I said, "let's try to contact the inhabitants. Anyplace with so much natural beauty must have intelligent life to appreciate it. The Phobosians surely will do everything in their power to welcome us."

"Take me to your leader," joked Adam.

We all agreed that the search for intelligent life should be our first order of business; but Troy was not so sure that the Phobosians would indeed be friendly. However, we soon cast such doubts to the wind, for Phobos was much too pretty to allow us to entertain morbid fears for long.

We set off in no particular direction. Everywhere we looked we saw the same lavender foliage; it was pleasant to gaze upon. I have often thought how dull green is and how unfortunate it is that green is the color of most of the Earth's vegetation. This opened up an area of speculation which I found fascinating.

"Suppose," I said, "that each world has its own particular personality. Now suppose that this personality is reflected by the color which dominates that world. Earth vegetation is mostly green, the color which symbolizes envy. Doesn't that fit in with the character of man? People fight petty wars and hate those who have more or are different."

"Well," said Troy thoughtfully, "that's an intriguing theory, Wart. But three-quarters of the Earth's surface is covered by water, which is blue. Now blue is a color I would associate with tragedy and, as I see it, tragedy is one of the inescapable facts of human existence."

"What nonsense you guys talk," put in Adam, but he went on listening interestedly.

So we strolled along—Christopher scurrying ahead of us— and we talked of such matters. Thus, we noticed the sound so gradually that at first it seemed merely background noise to our conversation. Suddenly, though, we were all aware of a buzzing.

"What's that?" asked Troy, turning around. Adam and I turned also, and we were confronted by an astonishing sight. Flying toward us, not forty feet away, was a swarm of giant bees the size of small elephants!

"Run!" shouted Troy. We all bolted off toward a cluster of purple trees which seemed to be the entrance to a forest. We had only run about one hundred yards when the bees overtook us and boxed us into a small circle. Frozen in fear, we heard one of the bees, apparently the leader, address us in a strange, lisping tongue. To my amazement, I understood the creature perfectly!

"From where do you come?" he asked.

I quickly perceived that the others could not understand the bee's question and surprised myself by answering in the same strange language:

"We come from the planet Earth, Mr. Giant Bee, and we are searching for the inhabitants of this world. Are there any such as us here?"

The bee regarded me intently. "No," he said, "there are none like you here. There are some like your two companions."

I explained to Troy and Adam what the bee had told me.

"Ask him if he can take us to a human city, then," said Troy.

I formulated this question to the giant bee of Phobos in that language I had never spoken, but somehow knew.

"A human city, eh?" lisped the bee. "Well, we are not on very friendly terms with the humans, but we will drop you off outside the modern cave city of Zertal. We have an—er—agreement with the Zertalians."

Several of the other bees appeared to snicker at these words. There was something in the leader bee's attitude that made me uneasy, but I could not quite place my snout on what it was.

I again interpreted for Troy and Adam.

"How will we get there?" asked Adam.

I put the question to the bee, who immediately responded, "You will fly there, of course, on our backs." He called out three names, and three bees came forward. We were directed to climb atop them, and we did as we were told, Adam scooping little Christopher up in his arms. A second later I felt a sticky substance flooding my hooves. When I tried to move my legs, I found them held fast in the bee's fur. It seemed that the bees could release this gluelike gook at will. I was held so firmly that had the bee turned upside down, I would have stayed in place.

We soon found ourselves flying high above the beautiful terrain. Had the circumstances been different I am sure the trip would have been fun, but I was worried with a fear I could not name. We flew for about two hours, straight and true, until we reached a group of cylindrical objects. At first I took them to be caves, but on closer inspection, I saw they were giant beehives!

We landed at the base of one of these structures and were pulled off the bees' backs.

"What is this place?" I asked with a sinking feeling.

"Why, it is your new home," laughed the head bee. "Fools! Did you really think we would deliver you into the hands of our sworn enemies, the Zertalians? You must believe us mad! You are now our prisoners—to be eaten at our next Feast of Death!"

In indignant anger we were herded through the twisting maze of upwardly spiraling corridors in what we soon learned was called the prison hive. Three bees followed us, hovering in the air and gliding forward, prodding us with spears and urging us to move faster. We passed up through maze after maze of fantastic hallways. They twisted to the right or left at every corner so often that in a matter of moments we were hopelessly lost. Our guards moved us cruelly forward and, after what seemed an eternity, we reached a vast empty platform in what I took to be the hive's center. The bees ordered us to mount their backs, and they took off, flying vertically upward so that I was forced to hang on for my life with my teeth.

As we flew upward, we passed level after level of the hive. We were evidently in its central shaft, through which, I guessed, all business was conducted aerially.

The bees beat their tortuous way upward. Finally we came to a level floor quite near the roof of the hive. The bees landed and ordered us down a hallway.

We passed many doorways, behind which we could hear horrible noises, until we reached the end of the hall. There, before an iron door, we saw an obese and ugly bee. He wore a belt around his middle into which was tucked a whip.

"More prisoners?" asked the fat bee.

"Yes, Stonar. To be eaten at the next Feast of Death!" said one of our captors.

"Indeed," the fat bee said, narrowing his eyes. I was aware that he was studying me. "And what manner of creature is this?"

"I do not know, Stonar."

The bee called Stonar was making motions with his mouth as though he were tasting some savory treat. "It should be good to eat," he said.

The bee who had spoken before seemed to shift his weight uneasily. "Perhaps, Stonar, you had best let Jarak take your place on guard duty. Too many unexplained accidents have been occurring in your sector. I would feel better if . . ."

"Quiet, fool!" shouted Stonar. "You are but a transport bee!

Do not forget your place! I will continue to look after my sector, as always."

The transport bee lowered his head. "Yes, Stonar," he said.

"You are dismissed," said Stonar. The three transport bees each made some strange type of salute and, one by one, flew off.

Stonar regarded us, particularly me, for some time. Then, chuckling to himself, he flew slowly over to a rack from which hung several keys. He took one and unlocked the door of our cell. With a majestic bow in mid-air, he motioned us inside. We seemed to have no choice but to obey, and so we entered. We heard the key turn in the door behind us and the vulgar sound of Stonar laughing to himself. I sensed that our troubles with him were just beginning.

Once inside the cell we looked around us. It was dimly lit and foul-smelling. There were human figures huddled in the corners. At first these figures appeared to be sleeping, but on closer inspection we found them to be, for the most part, awake. They lay as if drugged, gazing at us with uninterested eyes.

"Cheerful specimens," remarked Adam glumly.

I felt nearly as downhearted and depressed as most of our cellmates looked. "It would appear we are in a bit of a fix," I said.

"It looks that way, Wart," said Adam. "But tell us, how can you understand what these bees are saying? And talk their language? It sounds like gibberish to me."

"Well, Adam," I said, "I suppose that whatever higher power gave me the ability to speak the languages of Earth from the day of my birth also gave me this gift. It surprises me as much as it does you! But my abilities as a linguist won't get us out of this hive. We've got to think of something!"

Just then one of the prisoners stirred. He stood slowly and then approached us. I noticed that his skin gave off a lavender glow. So even the people were purple on Phobos!

"New prisoners for the Feast of Death," he said. It was more a statement than a question. He spoke in the same language as the bees.

"So we are told," I said.

"You know there is no escape."

"Perhaps not," I told him, sounding more courageous than I felt, "but we will die trying."

"You will die whether you try or not," said the young man. We were all silent for a while. Then the man from Phobos spoke again.

"Let me introduce myself. I am John-Doe of the forest city of Jig. And who might you be?"

Introductions were made all around, with me acting as a translator.

"What brings you to the land of the giant bees? Where do you come from? I have never seen your like on our world before."

"It is a long story," I said.

"Diversion comes not often to the prison hive," said our new-found friend. "Anyone with an interesting story to tell is appreciated, if only to break the ungodly monotony of waiting to die. So proceed with your tale, Mr. Warthog—for it will certainly be the last you are ever to tell!"

3

Escape and Capture

I related the bizarre incidents surrounding our arrival on Phobos to John-Doe. He pressed me to tell more about Earth, and I recounted what little I knew of it. I then reminded him that we knew next to nothing about Phobos.

"Phobos is spherically shaped and, from the measurements you have mentioned to me, much smaller than the Earth," began John-Doe, warming to his subject. "There are four major land masses which encompass about one-third of the planet; the rest is ocean. Spread throughout the land are the three major races of Phobos: the ghastly giant bees; humans, like myself; and a third race of hideous apelike creatures called Torks, much larger and more savage than your little friend" (here, he gestured at Christopher). "These roam about in primitive bands and eat human flesh.

"Of these three races, the humans are by far the most civilized. But each year our numbers are drastically reduced due to frequent raids by the bees and the Torks. Both of those races hate each other, which is fortunate for us humans; if they ever united against us, the results would be disastrous!"

"How many human cities still remain?" I asked.

"The last remnants of our race have taken refuge in two cities: the modern cave city of Zertal and the forest city of Jig."

I explained to Troy and Adam the conditions existing on Phobos, and they listened carefully. As I spoke, John-Doe appeared to slump back into dejection.

"Tell us, John-Doe," I said, "how did you come to be captured by the giant bees?"

He looked at the floor and hesitated before replying. "I came by myself to the land of the giant bees in the hope of finding the Princess Li-Narr, my betrothed. We suspected that she had been captured by the bees, and I . . ."

John-Doe's voice broke, and he turned away.

"Ahem . . . er," said Adam, clearing his throat. "Would you ask our friend here what this Feast of Death we are supposed to be the main course at is all about? If we are going to die, I'd like to know the reason!"

I put this question to John-Doe when he was calm again.

"Every six months," he said, "the bees honor their god, Kol-Dronn. On this occasion, all prisoners occupying the prison hive are eaten. The Queen Bee believes that the Feast is an incentive to the warrior bees to be ever alert for prisoners."

I heard the sound of a key turning in our cell door. Stonar

40

flew in, armed with a long, thin blade. Shutting the door behind him, he fixed me with his eyes and began flying slowly toward me.

"Every so often," said Stonar, slyly, "a prisoner makes an attempt to escape. When this happens, the guard cannot be blamed if he is forced to kill the prisoner. Then the guard may have the body to do with as he pleases. In the past month there have been five attempts to break out of my sector. Each prisoner has wound up on my dinner table. A moment ago I had a vision: in this vision I saw you, Creature, plotting a departure from the prison hive. Following that vision I had another: I saw my wife taking you from the oven, baked up very nicely, with a *pulva* fruit stuck in your mouth!" Stonar was now quite close to me.

"Stand fast, Creature!" he bellowed. "One move will be interpreted as an escape attempt!"

I stood stock-still for the next few minutes. Tension, fear, and anger mingled like an invisible mist in the cell. Stonar began to show signs of impatience. He suddenly pricked me with his sword, drawing blood from my right flank.

"Hey!" yelled Adam. "You can't do that!" With a wail of fury he leapt upon Stonar's back and began to pound him with his fists. I sprang up impulsively and attached my teeth to the belt which held the bee's weapons, jabbing my tusks into his belly. Although Stonar shrieked horribly and began squirming and tossing in an attempt to rid himself of us, both Adam and I held on fast and soon forced him to the ground. But before Troy could take Stonar's sword, the furious bee dealt me a savage cut just above my eyes.

"Stand fast, Creature," he bellowed. "One move will be interpreted as an escape attempt."

"That does it!" screamed Troy in rage, snatching the weapon from Stonar. He lifted the sword; then, looking around, he tossed it to one of the other prisoners.

The apathy of our Phobosian cellmates dissolved rapidly. Led by the man who had caught the weapon, the prisoners fell upon the deplorable hulk that was Stonar.

Blood from my wound flowed into my eyes, shutting out the grisly sight. My head began to spin; feeling weak and ill, I lapsed into unconsciousness.

When I awoke it was night, and a fire blazed in front of me. My head, wrapped in a cloth bandage, was propped up on a log. I had a headache, and the pain of the wound was great, though not unbearable. Raising my head slightly, I saw Troy, Adam, John-Doe, and Christopher squatting in a circle around the fire.

"Why, hello," I said, managing a faint smile. "How did I get here?"

At this, all heads turned in my direction. Gloomy expressions were replaced by wide grins. Even Christopher looked happy to see me awake.

"Hey," said Troy. "The hero is up! How do you feel, Wart?"

"Happy to be alive," I said truthfully. "What happened, though? The last I remember was the prisoners in the hive beating Stonar . . ."

". . . to death," finished Adam. "After you passed out, it seems that one of the bees patrolling the floor sounded an alarm. Soon the floor was swarming with bees. But the prisoners fought like madmen. We disarmed the bees, took their keys, and began unlocking other cells. Man, what a sight it was! Some of those poor guys went insane and jumped from the edge of the shaft to their deaths. Others mounted the bees and forced the beasts to transport them from floor to floor, fleeing other humans.

"Troy, John-Doe, and I managed to get you and Christopher onto the back of a big hulk of a bee. He was no menace at all—he shook all over at the sight of our swords. We made him carry all five of us down to the first level of the hive, and we got out of there as quickly as we could. That was several hours and a few miles back."

"Well!" I said. "I must thank you, for had it not been for your efforts, I would be dead, on my way to Stonar's wife's oven!"

"No," said Adam with a smile. "If it were not for you, Wart, we would all be someone's dinner!"

There was a silence as we all stared into the crackling flames, thinking our own thoughts.

"All the same," I said presently, "we're not out of the darkness yet. We must get John-Doe here safely home and ourselves back to Earth."

"Yeah," said Adam. "I like that last part, Wart. Back to Earth and sweet Janie. I hope she's not too mad. It'll probably take a dozen roses for her to forgive me for standing her up!"

"I agree with Wart," said Troy. "We certainly must get back to Earth and report this. What a scientific discovery! Life on Phobos!"

Adam rolled his eyes, laughing at Troy's excitement, but I remained silent. I thought back to the launching pad in Staten Island and the events which had brought us to this dangerous place. Was it not my differentness that had led us here? I had felt isolated from my own kind, so I had sought the company of human beings and been blessed with two fast friends. But no sooner had we ventured together into the outside world than there had been trouble—because I was a talking warthog, a most peculiar and, yes, freakish thing.

Thinking these despondent thoughts, I became aware that I was still very weary. Excusing myself, I rolled over and escaped into the world of sleep.

The next morning we decided we should first find our rocket to make sure no damage had been done. Then we would discuss how best to help our friend John-Doe in his search for his fiancée, Li-Narr.

So it was that we all set out. In the light of the new day, our situation did not seem so hopeless. Everyone except John-Doe was in high spirits. Christopher danced along ahead of us while Troy and I discussed matters that must be attended to when we reached the rocket. Adam, a loafer at heart, dragged along, inhaling the sweet air and admiring the luxuriant purple landscape as he blew a cheerful tune on his harmonica. John-Doe trailed along behind, looking very downcast, no doubt thinking of his missing Li-Narr. I had explained to him that we planned to help him in his quest and this had brightened him a bit, though not much.

In an hour we found an icy stream and drank deeply. The liquid tasted like water but was somehow more satisfying. John-Doe called it *asil* and bathed my wound with it, saying it had great healing power. He also introduced us to the pinkish fruit called *pulva*. It contained a nectar which one could suck on for hours without exhausting the supply. Its pleasant aftertaste left me feeling calm and refreshed for the entire day.

That night we made camp in a clearing and slept under the serene peace of the strange stars overhead. Whether it was the fruit, the water, or some miraculous Phobosian healing process I do not know, but when I awoke the next morning, the wound over my eyes was completely gone!

We forged ahead. About noon, Troy shouted that he recognized a landmark. It was a great stone outcropping, shaped like a man's hand, which he claimed he had noted while flying overhead on the back of one of our captor bees. We were much excited by this proof that we were headed in the right direction, and we followed Troy anxiously.

Troy was right. In a short time we sighted the rocket. As we drew near, I caught a foul scent in the air. A few moments later, my eye fell on what looked like the footprint of a huge ape. I called John-Doe's attention to it.

He examined the footprint with a frown. "That looks like a Tork track," he said to me. "We'd better be watchful."

We walked cautiously on, then stopped at the edge of the forest. John-Doe motioned for us to keep out of sight.

"The ship looks all right," said Adam, getting ready to step forward. Just then we heard a noise. Looking up, we saw the hatch open!

Standing framed in the doorway was an immense, hulking creature, at least seven feet tall, completely covered with matted, thick fur except around the eyes and mouth. Its only garment was a filthy loincloth. As it stood surveying us, I could see jagged, yellow fangs protruding from its half-open mouth I wrinkled my nose at the nasty odor that came from the beast.

"It's a Tork!" cried John-Doe. "Don't go any closer!" We stopped in terror.

"There must be more nearby," said John-Doe to me, "for they always travel in groups."

Unaware of the danger, Christopher ran forward and raced up the ladder leading to the hatchway. When he reached the top rung he simply dangled there, watching the Tork, who scowled down at him. Chattering happily, the monkey tapped the beast's foot and scampered down the ladder, looking over his shoulder, in an obvious effort to provoke a chase. He did this twice more, and the third time the Tork gave an ugly snarl and viciously kicked Christopher to the ground.

"You dumb apes!" Adam shouted. He rushed to the base of the ladder to examine Christopher, who was unconscious. The Tork started down the ladder with astonishing agility. Three more of the beasts, who had been hidden inside, followed him, and they stood in a group eyeing Adam and the monkey. Troy, John-Doe, and I advanced cautiously. By the time we reached them, Adam had gathered Christopher up in his arms and was glaring at the man-ape.

"You fellows play too rough," he said.

The Torks grunted to each other. Seeing we were in for trouble, I attempted to make peace with the creatures by telling John-Doe to give them some of the fruit we had brought with us. This the Torks greedily accepted. Instead of ensuring friendship, however, this action served quite the opposite purpose. When they learned we had no more to offer, the Torks grew sulky and began to growl.

Things looked bad. I must admit I was frightened by these hulking ape-men. "What should we do?" I asked Troy.

"I know a little bit about how these types think," said Troy. "You've got to handle them firmly but gently, like a bad child. Watch."

He stepped forward and put his hand on the arm of one of the Torks. "Okay, big fella. You've had your fun. Now I think you'd better be moving . . ."

In the next instant Troy was sprawling on the ground. The ape who had struck him snarled savagely.

"Nice going, Troy," said Adam. Then the other Torks began to close in on us.

Adam, John-Doe, and I leapt at an ape-creature apiece, but they flung us from them as a man might fling away a scrap of paper blown into his face on a windy day. Soon we were all lying on the ground, trying to protect ourselves from the Torks' blows. Growling to each other, the beasts pulled us to our feet and began pushing us toward a thick forest, leaving poor Christopher on the lavender grass beneath the *Helena 1*.

4
The Village of Death

It was dusk when at last we stumbled, bruised and battered, into the village of the Torks of Phobos. As we were led through the dusty streets, Torks stared silently at us. At one end of the village, I caught a glimpse of a peculiarly carved, hideous idol, and it caused my tail to rise. Before I was able to study it very well, our captors shoved us into a stone hut.

The interior of the hut was plain and foul-smelling. Its only other occupant, a striking young woman with flaming red hair framing her lavender face, looked up as we entered.

"John-Doe!" she screamed excitedly.

John-Doe's eyes widened in astonishment. "Li-Narr!" he cried and ran into her arms.

For a full minute they embraced passionately, leaving the rest of us somewhat embarrassed. Then they turned toward us, smiling in that shy, innocent way lovers have in the presence of others.

"Mr. Warthog and friends," John-Doe announced, "may I introduce you to the most beautiful woman on Phobos—or any other world. She is Li-Narr, princess of the forest city of Jig and my future wife."

We all bowed graciously, and I introduced Troy and Adam to Li-Narr. Then we squatted on the ground and made ourselves as comfortable as possible. John-Doe and Li-Narr held hands as she began to tell how she came to be a prisoner of the disgusting Torks.

"Well," she said, "I had become bored with royal life and felt I needed some excitement. I begged my father, King Ronk-Gorr, to let me venture outside the city gates to the forest land beyond. My father, John-Doe will tell you, is a kind and wise man, though perhaps a bit overprotective, and he denied me his permission. I was not to be stopped, and I slipped out of the city one night dressed as a peasant woman. My intention was to spend one or two days in the wild before returning home to face my punishment. But the first day, as I stood in a field picking berries, several giant bees spied me. They were almost upon me when a group of Torks came out of the forest, hurling stones at the bees. They drove the bees away and took me prisoner.

"They marched me for three miserable days to reach this desolate place. Those were the most terrible days I have ever experienced! The beasts marched me day and night, stopping only for food and water, very little of which they gave me. The third day they dragged me into this hut. I believe we are being kept prisoners for some sacrificial rite, for I caught glimpses of strange altars and a terrible idol of some sort."

50

"Yes," I said in Phobosian. "I noticed the idol, too."

I turned to Troy and Adam and related Li-Narr's tale in English.

"Man!" exclaimed Adam. "It looks like life on Phobos is just out of the frying pan and into the fire. To be sacrificed and eaten by giant bees or seven-foot apes—what's the difference, Wart?"

"Very little, I must agree," I said. "But we are still alive, and John-Doe here has found his beloved, so all is not totally grim. Let us try to get some sleep; things always look better in the daytime."

Shortly thereafter I drifted off into a fitful slumber which was disturbed by a peculiarly vivid dream. In my dream I was back in the bush, running from a group of angry warthogs led by Horgor. It seemed I had committed some terrible crime against the tribe. Looking over my shoulder, I saw them gaining on me. Then the running warthogs turned into running Torks, and Horgor into the idol I had seen. They began to gibber and scream, and I awoke with a start to the same gibbering and screaming. But this was real. There was some kind of commotion going on outside our hut. I heard much growling and the sound of Torks rushing furiously about. My companions were also awake, peering around in a state of confusion.

"Something's happening," said Troy. All five of us crowded into the doorway of the hut and gazed outside. There was no guard to be seen. Stepping out I saw, at the far end of the village, what looked like the entire tribe of Torks. They were throwing stones at a small brown figure dancing among the branches of a tree.

"It's Christopher!" shouted Adam in delight. "He must have recovered and followed us!"

As we watched, a few of the Torks started to climb the tree, but Christopher quickly swung through the branches, resuming his taunting several yards away. He dodged sticks and stones alike, confounding the slow-witted Torks.

"Quick!" I whispered. "We must act while there's time!"

We all bolted toward the forest's edge, opposite the place where the apes were congregated. We reached the cover of the purple vegetation and lay flat in the underbrush.

"Look here," said Adam. "We can't just run off and leave Christopher behind. You guys try to reach the rocket, and I'll stay back and try to save my little buddy."

"I'll assist you, Adam," I said.

"Well," said Troy, logically, "It would do no good for all of us to stay here and attempt the rescue. If John-Doe, Li-Narr, and I head back to the rocket, we could be ready to go when you guys arrive with Christopher." With those words we split up, Adam and I circling through the underbrush while our companions hastily made their way toward the rocket.

Christopher was still teasing the Torks when Adam and I stopped and hid behind a large knoll. We could hear their ghastly shrieks and growls and the gleeful noises Christopher made as he maneuvered skillfully among the trees. We had had no time to discuss a plan, but acting on a sudden impulse, I sprang atop the knoll and called out to the Torks in the language of African warthogs. Surprised, the apes turned in my direction. Taking advantage of their momentary confusion, Adam silently raced to

52

Christopher's tree and attracted the monkey's attention. After Christopher had dropped lithely to Adam's shoulder, Adam wheeled and raced off into the forest. A split second later, I followed suit.

Realizing they had been tricked, the Torks quickly took up the chase. Their yells raised a tremendous hubbub throughout the peaceful forest. I caught up with Adam, and we raced along at a fast clip. At one point I chanced a glance over my shoulder, and the sight which met my eyes filled me with fear and loathing: the Torks were swinging through the trees *above* us at a frenzied pace. Perhaps it was the angle at which I saw them, or perhaps it was the savage look of determination carved upon their faces, but at that moment those beasts seemed the most shocking monstrosities I had ever beheld.

They say that fear lends wings to the feet, and I can testify to the truth of that statement. I ran as I had never run before. My four legs pumped like quicksilver, and my heart and head pounded like the drum of a crazed soloist. My breath came in spurts, and I was sure that at any second I would drop from exhaustion. Still I shot ahead of Adam. I glanced back, but before I could see anything, I slammed into something hard and warm. I was sent spinning into darkness.

I could not have been unconscious for more than a minute. When I opened my eyes, a great golden beast was towering over me. It was like a horse (though larger), but its head resembled a lion's, down to its shaggy mane. I stared up into its dusty gray eyes, and it stared down into mine.

I was preparing to surrender myself to its jaws when I noticed that the beast wore a collar. So it was tame! Perhaps its owner was nearby.

Looking around, I spotted Adam and the monkey a short distance away. Adam was panting and watching the horse-lion with puzzled eyes. I looked over my shoulder and saw no sign of the Torks.

"It's tame," I said.

"Yes," wheezed Adam, coming toward me. "What luck! It stepped out of that cave suddenly, and the Torks turned tail and fled at the sight of it. It looks friendly enough, though," he said, stroking the creature's mane cautiously. Christopher seemed to be suffering no ill effects from our run, for he was engaged in a game of hide and seek with some small rodent of Phobos.

"It somewhat resembles a horse," I said. "Perhaps it is a riding beast."

Adam's eyes became bright. "Yeah," he said, still breathing heavily. "That would be super-duper. As beat as we are, we could use a ride to the rocket on the back of this beast! Let's take a rest first, though; I'm pooped. With its help we can still get back at the same time as the others."

Keeping a sharp lookout for Torks, we sat for a good hour in the Phobosian wilderness, getting our strength back. Then Adam stood and began stroking the odd creature that had frightened the Torks away. He scrambled up onto the animal's back, and it seemed not to mind the passenger.

"Climb aboard, Wart," said Adam. "We've got a ride! Hi-ho, Silver! Or maybe I should say 'Gold'?"

With Adam's assistance, I managed to reach the creature's

back. There I squatted precariously, clutching Adam's shirttail in my mouth. Adam directed the beast to move, and we were off. He guided it by gently tugging its mane. The ride was a bit bouncy for me, but we reached the rocket in a little under an hour, following landmarks we had noted on our previous excursion through the forest to the village of the Torks.

As we approached the *Helena 1,* Troy, John-Doe, and Li-Narr waved to us from its base.

"So!" Troy exclaimed. "The saviours return! I was beginning to worry a bit. But where did this beastie come from?"

"That is a wild morr," said John-Doe; "but this one isn't so wild, for it wears a collar!"

I explained to Troy what had occurred in the short time since we had last seen them. He whistled.

"Well," he said, "I just finished taking a quick look at the rocket before you came riding up, and everything's in tip-top shape. The Torks must not have had a chance to damage anything. We can leave Phobos any time, and there's still enough food and water on the ship to last us until we reach Earth."

We all stood silent for a while. Though he could not understand Troy's words, I am sure John-Doe understood their meaning.

"It was an honor to know you all," said the Phobosian. "But I think we must part now, for Li-Narr and I must find City Jig. We can use this morr, for I am very good at riding them. Perhaps, someday, our paths will cross again."

I translated this speech for Adam and Troy, and we all wished the two Phobosians well. Li-Narr gave me the sweetest kiss on my forehead, telling John-Doe I was "cute." Troy and Adam exchanged that universal gesture of friendship, the handshake, with John-Doe. Moments later, we were ascending the ladder to the rocket, waving goodbye.

Once inside, Adam breathed a sigh. "Well, homeward bound, I guess," he said. "Quick, Troy, let's lift off before some other carnivorous guys try to put us on their menu!"

Troy threw some switches, and the rocket began to quake. I felt a little sad to be leaving John-Doe and Li-Narr, for I had just begun to know and like them. I hoped they would find their way home safely. As we lifted off, I glanced out of a viewport and saw the two figures, hand in hand, waving at us. They looked like such a pretty couple. It made me wonder if somewhere, on some world, there was a creature to love me as she loved him.

5
Trouble in Karobia

The return journey to Earth went smoothly. We made good use of our weeks in space to rest and recover from the whirlwind events of our few days on Phobos. But it was in my nature to fret, and toward the end of our trip, I began to have fears about what would happen when we reached America again. Remembering the angry and distrustful guards who had frightened me into leaping aboard the *Helena 1*, I was afraid that the U.S. government's attitude might be similarly hostile. I might be arrested and put in jail for the rest of my life! My friends accepted me as I was, but what if the rest of the human race thought like those guards? For some reason I found myself thinking of the wise old warthog Zareemba. He had told me it was wonderful to be different. Could he be right? I decided to trust him (what else could I do?) and let things work themselves out.

When we entered the Earth's gravitational field, the *Helena 1* began to quiver and shake in a most distressing manner. Troy bounded over to the console and began making frantic adjustments. "How could I be so dumb?" he said out loud.

"What's wrong?" I asked.

"As well-designed as this ship is, it was never meant to travel so great a distance with our additional weight. The wear and tear has been too much for it. If we don't land soon, the entire ship will fall apart!"

"What are our chances?" asked Adam.

"Slim," answered Troy, solemnly. "I have now adjusted the controls so that we are headed toward a body of water somewhere near India. This will be close, guys. If we don't hit water, it's all over!"

The rocket was plummeting at a sickening rate. It passed through a cluster of clouds, into the blueness of Earth's sky, and then we splashed down in water.

We had all been tossed off balance by the force of the landing, but there was no doubt we were safe. I looked through the viewport and saw water settling under it. Troy looked out of the viewport, then turned to us with a grin. "I can hardly believe it, but it seems we have landed in a natural water basin. It's just deep enough to have stopped the ship's fall, but not deep enough to totally immerse it!"

"Great!" Adam exclaimed. He pulled out his harmonica and began playing a joyful tune, stamping his feet. I clapped my hooves to the music, laughing with delight. Even the serious Troy grabbed Christopher and did a little dance with him. After about

58

a minute of this, Adam pocketed his instrument and rushed to the hatchway to open it. When he touched the latch, he jumped back with a yowl.

"Whew!" he said, nursing his hand. "That door is hot!"

"Yes," said Troy, "and the heat from reentry is spreading rapidly to other parts of the rocket. We'd better get out!"

As Troy opened the hatch with a control lever, water came tumbling in, forcing us back. Troy scooped me up on his shoulders. Little Christopher squatted atop Adam, and the boys exited from the hatchway and began swimming. The water surrounding the *Helena 1* was very hot, and Troy kicked out for the nearby shore. I paddled along next to him. We reached shore shortly after Adam and Christopher and sat by the water, breathing heavily. The outer hull of the rocket was cracking rapidly, and soon chunks of metal began to fall into the water.

"You did it, Troy!" Adam sighed with relief.

I looked at our new surroundings. Although we had only been on Phobos a little while, it seemed odd to see greenery again. The brink of the basin where we sat was surrounded by lush tropical growth. I could sense the presence of unseen life scurrying through the bushes about us.

"You say we are somewhere near India?" I asked Troy.

"Yes," he replied. "By my calculations we are at longitude . . ."

We were interrupted by a sound behind us, or rather behind me. Troy sat facing me, and I saw his jaw drop and his eyes widen as he peered at something above my head. I turned and found myself staring down the inside of a rifle barrel!

I gasped as my eyes took in the rifle and its owner. The fellow had dark brown skin, and his hair and beard were jet black. He wore a turban, and his feet were shod in sandals. His clothes consisted only of a simple, togalike white garment. His handsome face was young; he looked not more than twenty.

"Good day, sir," I said, pretending not to notice that the rifle pointed directly at my head. Behind me, Troy and Adam mumbled greetings.

"Who are you?" asked the bearded fellow in English.

We introduced ourselves cordially, but still he pointed the rifle.

"Where have you come from? And what were you doing in that craft?" He gestured toward the ruin of the *Helena 1* in the middle of the water basin.

"We will certainly tell you, sir," I said, "if you would but lower your rifle."

The bearded Indian looked skeptical, but at last he turned the gun down. I noticed, though, that his finger still rested on the trigger.

I outlined how Troy, Adam, myself, and Christopher had come to be passengers on the *Helena 1* and briefly explained the events on Phobos and our return trip to Earth. He appeared fascinated and soon set the rifle on the ground.

"Yes," he said in charmingly accented English, "I have heard much of the astounding science of America."

"That's right," spoke up Troy proudly. "It's the most advanced nation in the world scientifically, you know!" Adam snorted at Troy's enthusiasm, but said nothing.

"I am most sorry to have greeted you so rudely," said the Indian. "I was hunting when I sighted your rocket falling from the sky. I rushed here thinking you might be invaders. But allow me to introduce myself; perhaps you have heard my name. I am Prince Hasaami of Karobia."

I exchanged glances with Troy and Adam. We had read about the unfortunate prince in the newspapers just before our voyage. The story ran that King Samyra of Karobia, a small, somewhat backward country near India, had been killed by rebels. In his place on the throne now was a man named Bas-Raay, by all accounts an unscrupulous dictator with a tremendous lust for power. King Samyra's only son, Hasaami, had been spared his father's fate and "allowed" to live the life of a poor man in the city.

"I can see by your faces that you've heard of the affair," said Hasaami with a sour smile. "Yes, I am he. The rightful ruler of Karobia—forced to live as a poor man!" With a disgusted shrug he slung the rifle over his shoulder. "I imagine you will be in need of some kind of shelter," Hasaami continued. "If you wish you may return with me to my humble home. I am staying in a baker's shop, where I make my living baking bread. Of course, there is little money to be made, for Bas-Raay taxes the people unmercifully. He is cruel, and everyone fears him. Well, my new-found friends, if you will follow me I will try to make your stay with me comfortable."

We walked through some jungle and in a short time reached the city. Prince Hasaami led us to his hut, which was in the most run-down section of Karobia. The city was an odd mixture of the rural and the urban. Small shacks stood side by side with ten-story buildings. There hung over everything that air of fear and uneasiness that one feels in a conquered nation.

Hasaami took us to a tiny room at the back of the shop and brought us some bread and tea. (The bread was the finest I have ever tasted, I might add.) As we ate, he talked with us.

"Before my father was murdered, he had great hopes for his people. He looked forward to the day when Karobia would be a prosperous nation, and the people would be proud. But now!" He pounded his fist on the table, leapt up, and began to pace angrily about the little room. "With that jackal upon the throne, there is no hope for Karobia. To satisfy his corrupt and lavish tastes, he would let the people starve! His latest outrage is to build a huge, ultramodern addition to my father's palace to house his harem of wives! It makes my blood boil! I remember often my father would weep in rage and sadness at the sight of a hungry man begging in the street!"

So moved were we by the prince's speech that we sat in silence for several minutes. Then, with an air of great weariness, Prince Hasaami spoke again.

"Well, there is no use in dreaming now. You must be quite tired from your long journey. You will find blankets in that cabinet there. Sleep well, my friends; tomorrow you will witness a sight to make you wish you had never awakened!" And with those cryptic words, Hasaami took leave of us.

As we were getting ready for bed, Adam asked. "What do you make of this tragedy, Wart?"

"It's an ugly state of affairs," I answered. "But the prince's

62

spirit is not broken yet. Perhaps it will all work out in the long run."

"I think we should help him!" exclaimed Adam. "The people are too scared to rebel, and one man can't stand against a dictatorship."

"Right now," I said, "I think we should all try to rest, for judging by our friend's words, tomorrow should prove to be most interesting." That night, however, I lay awake for a long time thinking before sleep finally overcame me. It occurred to me that there were far worse things than being different. I was luckier than I had ever thought. I had my freedom. My parents were both alive and well, and I had not one-quarter of the heartache that poor Hasaami had. Although we might be in danger, I felt better than I had in a long time.

We rose early the next morning and found Prince Hasaami at a table in the outer room. He was in a dark mood. He greeted us curtly, and we breakfasted on toast and tea.

"What's on the agenda today, Prince?" asked Troy, trying to sound casual.

"Today is the day the people gather to honor their great ruler," said Hasaami, his voice thick with bitter sarcasm. "Once a week it is required that all the citizens of Karobia gather in the marketplace to pay tribute to Bas-Raay and bring him gifts. We must go there now, but I will tell you there is nothing but hatred in my heart for Bas-Raay. That is my only 'gift' to him!"

We set out for the marketplace after finishing our tea. As we walked along, I noticed many people traveling in our direction, bearing trinkets, cakes, and such. Their faces were set in fixed, stony expressions, tinged with sorrow. It was a disturbing sight. I averted my eyes from them, gazed downward, and plodded on.

In fifteen minutes we reached the marketplace, a large area of tents and closed-down shops. There must have been thousands of people now gathered in the wide-open space that had been cleared in its center. We pushed our way through the crowd and stood in a spot quite close to where Hasaami told us Bas-Raay would appear.

After we had waited nearly an hour, the king was announced. People applauded joylessly. A few bold souls even booed, but Hasaami stood silent, not moving a muscle. He stared coldly ahead. Four husky manservants carried Bas-Raay on a couch hung with silk curtains. They set their burden down and drew back the curtains.

From where I stood, I had a fairly good view of him. The king was a grotesque sight. He looked as if he weighed three hundred pounds. His eyes were narrow and cruel, and his skin and hair were covered with a slimy film. He lay back on gaily colored silk pillows, puffing on a foot-long cigar. I shuddered in disgust, for knowing that he sat where he did because of murder made him doubly repulsive to behold.

"All will now kneel before the glory of the magnificent King Bas-Raay!" screamed a manservant.

The people, including Hasaami, sank to their knees. Out of the whole crowd only Troy, Adam, myself, and Christopher remained standing. From his kneeling position Prince Hasaami glanced at us. His eyes became wide when he saw us upright.

"Kneel!" he urged us in a frantic whisper.

The king's eyes were narrow and cruel, and his skin and hair were covered with a slimy film.

"Why?" I asked.

"Kneel!" he hissed again. "The failure to do so means your deaths!" By now two of the king's guards were making their way back toward us.

"Why do you not kneel before the might of King Bas-Raay?" one shrieked at Troy and Adam, who could not understand their language. I answered for them in Karobian:

"Why should we honor a false king?"

At this the two jumped back, looking astonished. Then their shock turned to anger.

"We shall see what the king has to say about this," the first guard snarled. "Of course, the penalty for such insolence is death, but I think a talking pig would greatly amuse His Majesty." Drawing long blades, the guards urged us toward the couch.

A long line of people stood before the king, offering a gift of some sort at his feet. One woman presented him with her daughter, a beautiful young girl with long black hair. The king instructed her to kiss his feet. "If I find the touch of her lips pleasing," said Bas-Raay, knocking the ash from his cigar, "I will spare her life." I watched in horror as the girl knelt and performed the deed.

"That is fine," said Bas-Raay, after a moment of consideration. "Now if her lips are as soft against my mouth as they are against my feet, I will consider making her one of my wives. Come, wench," he grinned terribly, displaying a row of uneven yellow teeth. "You may have the pleasure of kissing the great King Bas-Raay!" He puckered his lips and closed his eyes. As the girl leaned forward to kiss the king, I turned in disgust.

"Ah," sighed the king a moment later. "You will do, my dear. I . . ."

"Your Most Gracious Majesty, pardon for the interruption," spoke one of the guards who had brought us forward. "But we have a group of offenders here who refuse to kneel before your glory. One is a hog that talks!"

"Eh? What kind of creature is this?" he asked, addressing one of the guards but looking directly at me.

"I am a warthog," I spoke up boldly.

"What is it that you and your friends do in Karobia? And why do you not kneel? Perhaps you do not understand the seriousness of your offence!"

"We are here as guests of the true king of Karobia—Hasaami—and we do not kneel before murderers!" I answered angrily.

At my words the king's eyes grew wide, and he rose heavily.

"Off with his head!" he cried, sputtering in rage.

The two guards came toward me, each with blade drawn. Both lifted their weapons over their heads. At the last second, I ran swiftly between the first one's legs, butting him with my rear flank. A roar went up from the kneeling crowd. The guards wheeled about with howls of rage and rushed at me again. Adam snatched up a handful of dirt and hurled it into the face of the foremost guard, who began screaming and reached up to rub his eyes; the other collided with his comrade, and they both fell into a heap. I leapt forward and sank my teeth into the wrist of the first guard. He yelped in pain and dropped his sword, which Adam swiftly retrieved. Troy was quick to relieve the second man of his weapon, and the three of us turned to face the king.

"Fools!" screamed the king at his guards. "They are but two boys and a beast! You cannot allow this!" He beckoned to his manservants, who drew their own weapons.

From beside me I heard the voice of Hasaami, who had come forward during the skirmish. "Quickly," he said, "a sword. I am well schooled in the use of these!"

Adam handed Hasaami his blade. The prince wielded it with both hands, lifting it high above his head. "For King Samyra, my father!" he cried, advancing to meet the four burly manservants.

What followed can only be described as slaughter. Despite the four-to-one odds, Hasaami bested his opponents, fighting with more savagery than I had ever seen in any man. Within the space of a few minutes, three of the swordsmen were badly wounded and unable to fight. The fourth threw down his weapon and fled into the audience. Hasaami picked up the castaway blades and distributed them to four men in the crowd. Then he approached Bas-Raay, who was hiding under his cushions, trembling in fear and fury.

Hasaami threw the cushions aside and regarded the man who had arranged the murder of his father. Holding his weapon at Bas-Raay's neck, he asked in a controlled tone, "Do you surrender?"

For answer, the trembling man began begging the crowd to stop Hasaami. Not surprisingly, no one came forward.

The prince repeated his question.

Bas-Raay began to cry and beg for mercy.

"The same mercy you showed my father," said Hasaami. "You devil!" He slapped Bas-Raay full in the face. The ex-monarch tumbled from his couch and lay whimpering on the ground while the four swordsmen surrounded him.

The crowd was in a state of uproar. Hasaami turned toward his countrymen and, with a gesture, quieted them. He began to speak, saying a great deal about his gratitude to me and the boys for our courage. Then he said something that astonished me: he called for me to be hailed as the new king of Karobia. The crowd applauded enthusiastically, and I stepped forward quickly and addressed them in a loud voice.

"My dear friends," I said, "this will not do at all. As great an honor as it is to be offered kingship of your nation, I cannot accept. For one, I am not qualified. For another, it is not my right as I was not born into the royal family. But I will turn you back to the man who possesses both of these qualities: Prince . . . er . . . King Hasaami!"

A great cheer went up. King Hasaami smiled and bowed to me and turned again to address his people. He spoke of his plans for the future of Karobia and of what a monumental day it had been, but I believe this opening statement spoke volumes:

"People of Karobia," said he, "we are free!"

6
Poachers!

A few days later we decided to leave Karobia and King Hasaami. Bas-Raay had been imprisoned and was awaiting trial, and the king was going about the business of rebuilding the government. Hasaami had been very kind to us, giving us each a beautifully furnished room in his palace. He offered to let us stay as long as we wanted. However, we all knew we should head home as quickly as possible, and we told this to Hasaami. He arranged for us to be taken to the nearest airport, where his personal pilot, Alhazred, would fly us to America. Troy had sent a cable to Aunt Aramantha telling her that he and Adam were safe and would be home soon.

Looking out the airplane window, I realized that it had been almost two months since that fateful day we had visited the rocket base in Staten Island. The thought of our adventures left me pretty well amazed. I had surprised myself by attacking Stonar and standing up to the guards in Karobia. It was hard to believe that back in the bush I had let myself be pushed around by Horgor and the others. Things would be very different now, I thought, if I ever returned to Africa.

As if he had read my thoughts, Alhazred, a friendly fellow, told us it would be necessary to stop off in Africa to refuel and have some minor repair work done. It would take about a day or so, he said.

"What part of Africa will we be landing in?" I asked.

When he told me my heart began racing, for we would be very near the village of my tribe!

After some consideration I said to Troy and Adam, "Since we'll be in Africa for a short while, I wonder if you'd mind terribly if I slipped off to visit my parents?"

"We certainly would mind!" said Adam emphatically.

I looked puzzled until he added with a laugh, "That is, if you don't take us along with you. I would love to meet your folks, Wart!"

"Me, too," added Troy.

I grinned. "Then it's settled. You'll come with me, and I know they'll be happy to meet you both. I can think of no better companions in all the world!"

"Aw, shucks," said Troy. We all laughed.

It was daybreak when our plane landed near the western coast of Africa, not more than six miles from my birthplace. Indeed, we were very near the harbor where half a year ago I had met Troy and Adam. We told Alhazred that we would be back that evening. After stopping in the airport lounge for a bite to eat, we set off on foot through the bush, leaving Christopher behind with Alhazred.

It took us almost four hours to reach my village. I could have gotten there in one-third the time, but the boys weren't used to walking in the jungle. As we trooped into the village of my birth, I was filled with mixed emotions. I felt as though I had been away for years rather than months.

One of the first warthogs I saw was Jack Ham. When he saw me, he grunted in surprise.

I greeted Jack warmly and asked about his parents and his sister. He told me they were fine. He seemed a little startled to see me in the company of two human beings, but he stood and talked with me. All around us, warthogs had scuttered off into hiding at the sight of the boys. I chuckled to myself when I caught a glimpse of Horgor, peering out fearfully from behind a tree. Feeling mischievous, I called out to him in English.

"No need to be afraid, Horgor. They're friendly." It was the first time I had ever spoken in a human tongue among my kind.

Jack Ham gave me an odd look, then smiled. I started trotting to my parents' home, gesturing with my head for Jack and the boys to follow. Stopping in front of my parents' hut, I called to them. After a moment, my mother came out.

At the sight of me, she rushed over, lavishing me with kisses and questions, while Troy and Adam stood by shyly. I introduced the boys to her (in English), and she greeted them warmly. Then, pleading with us to make ourselves comfortable, she ran off to fetch fruit and water.

When she came back, she implored me to tell her all that had happened since she had last seen me. She spoke English, in low tones, looking at my companions in wonder every now and then. As I told her of my adventures, she sat listening, spellbound.

"My dear son," she said when I finished. "You should write a book! It is a great thing to have been the first warthog on another world and to have almost been a king!"

"Perhaps I will write a book someday, Mother," I replied. "But tell me, where is Father?"

No sooner had I spoken these words than I heard a grunt off to my left. Turning, I saw my father walking toward us. He looked exactly as I remembered him: distinguished, with tufts of gray about his ears. He moved with pride and grace, beaming at me with every step.

"My son!" he called, when he had come closer. "I thought it was you! It's wonderful to look at you again!"

I was about to introduce him to Troy and Adam when I caught the scent of men close by. I saw that my father smelled them also. We looked at each other, worried.

All of a sudden the village seemed to come to life as a group of men, swinging heavy poles and screaming, came running out of the jungle. Two or three ran to where we sat outside my parents' hut. Before we could move, they threw a large wire net over me, my parents, and Jack Ham.

"Hey, what's this?" yelled Adam, leaping up. A burly man pulled a blackjack from the pocket of his safari jacket and, with a sickening blow, knocked Adam unconscious.

"My brother!" screamed Troy. "You creeps!" But an instant later Troy, too, was socked on the head and fell to the ground.

In a tangle we were dragged by two men across the earth and thrown onto the back of a truck. I tried desperately to get out of the net, but my efforts were futile. Each movement drew the meshes tighter. I told my parents and Jack to keep still because struggling would only make things worse.

I saw men dragging more netted warthogs to other trucks nearby. A white-haired man with an eyepatch and a gun leaned against the back of our truck.

"Hey," I shouted. "What's the meaning of this?"

He wheeled and looked at me nervously. "Who said that?" he asked.

"I did," I answered. "What's the idea?"

"Well, well," he said. "A talking warthog! We'll make a fortune off you! Walsh said he met a man once who told him he'd seen one, but I thought it was hogwash. I guess it ain't. Any more like you in the batch?"

"No," I lied, thinking of my parents.

"It doesn't matter. We can sell the others to zoos or restaurants. Warthog steaks, haw! But you . . ." His one eye glistened. "You'll fetch a pretty penny for sure!"

So these men were poachers—common thieves. The thought enraged me. Another netful of warthogs was thrown on the truck.

"You'll never get away with this," I said to the one-eyed man.

"Who says? There's money in wild animals. Last week we sold a two-headed giraffe to a freak show. No one cares if we take a few animals out of Africa and make some bucks in the process. Well, looks like we're ready to leave. Don't go away now." Chuckling, he got in the truck beside the driver, then turned so he could see us. There was no window between us, and I heard him tell the driver that they had captured a talking warthog. The driver made a comment I couldn't hear, and both laughed as the truck pulled out. Mingled with the sound of the motor were the grunts and moans of helpless warthogs.

When I twisted my body in an attempt to get comfortable, the wire mesh bit into me painfully. My brain was racing. In less than fifteen minutes, these villains had captured my entire tribe, close to 160 warthogs. There were about 25 warthogs in my truck alone. Where were they taking us? How could we escape?

I calmed myself by breathing deeply. I saw that most of the other warthogs had also discovered that the best way to avoid pain was to stay still. I noticed the man with the eyepatch watching me with a sly smile.

"I see your friends have calmed down," he called. "Tell them to relax and enjoy the ride."

I ignored him, which seemed to make him angry.

"What, are you too good to talk to me?" he said. "Why don't you entertain the others with some jokes? No? Then I'll tell one." The fellow then told a story so lewd that I shuddered with distaste. When he finished he broke out in a fit of laughter. I remained silent, distressed that my mother had to hear his vulgarity. When he saw he would get no response from me, he grew quiet and said nothing else for the rest of the ride.

After a half hour, the truck ground to a halt behind another one filled with warthogs and poachers. We were unloaded—none too gently—and freed from our nets. I looked around. Six or seven more full trucks were pulling up. I asked my parents if they were all right. They nodded, though both looked frightened and confused to me.

I noticed we were near a pier where a battered old ship was docked. Many large wooden crates stood on the pier. I watched as two muscular men pried the top off one and threw three or four warthogs inside.

The white-haired man with the eyepatch was whispering to a bald man who carried a large bullwhip. I could tell they were talking about me. The man with the whip came and looked at me intently. I returned his stare.

"You can talk?" he asked brusquely.

"No," I said nastily. "It's done by ventriloquism."

I felt the harsh sting of the whip on my back. I braced myself for another blow, still looking at the bald man. But the gleam of anger in his eyes vanished like an extinguished candle, and he lowered the whip.

"That was stupid of me," he said. "Not that I care about you, but you are a very valuable little beastie, the only one of this bunch worth anything. The old ones will be destroyed, and the young ones sold. But you're a gold mine! Johnson, lock this one in the ship's cabin! Aside from his being the only talking warthog, his intelligence makes him dangerous."

The one-eyed man came toward me, holding a pistol which was aimed at my head. I backed away slowly.

Jack Ham, who had been standing near me, had begun to growl softly. As Johnson advanced, Jack Ham uttered his first sentence in English! His voice was extremely gruff-sounding, but his words came across loud and clear.

76

He said, "Stand back, or you'll be sorry!"

The bald man laughed loudly. "It seems we now have two valuable porkers! Wilson, Cullen—give Johnson a hand."

Two more poachers came forward. Jack Ham leapt up quickly, colliding with Johnson, who fired a wild shot before falling to the ground with Jack on top of him. The other two dragged Jack from their companion and knocked him senseless with their fists. One of them then heaved Jack's body onto his shoulder and carried him off in the direction of the ship.

Johnson, his face a bright red, climbed to his feet and pointed his pistol at me.

"Will you come quietly, or do I have to shoot?" he said angrily.

"You would not shoot me, for I am too valuable," I responded.

"Maybe so," he said, grinning evilly. "But for each minute you refuse to obey me, one of your warthog friends will die." He pointed his gun at a big warthog, whom I saw was Horgor, my old enemy. Horgor began to squeal and grunt in terror.

Even though I had no love for Horgor, there was nothing for me to do but surrender. My captors led me aboard the ship. They locked me in a small, damp room beneath the deck, binding my legs together before leaving me. It was dark, but gradually I made out the shape of Jack Ham lying near me, still unconscious. I settled myself back as best I could and waited for him to wake up. At the same time, I tried to come up with a plan of action. I recalled the head poacher's statement that the old warthogs would be destroyed; even now my parents and Old Zareemba might be on the brink of death! The thought filled me with dread.

After a while I heard the sounds of the other warthogs being loaded onto the ship. I heard a key in the lock and twisted in my bonds to see who it was. Johnson entered the room.

"My parents," I choked. "Have they been killed?"

"Huh? Oh, you mean the old ones. Not yet. When we get out to sea, we'll weigh them down with lead balls and chains and toss them overboard. No evidence. Clever, huh?" He snickered.

I breathed a sigh of mixed relief and despair; at least they were still alive, and where there is life, there is also hope.

Johnson opened a drawer in a corner of the cabin and took out a bottle of something that smelled like liquor. He took several greedy gulps and thrust the bottle back in the drawer. Emitting a belch, he turned and left, slamming the door after him.

My head was pounding, and I closed my eyes in pain. I lost track of the time and must have drifted off into a fitful half-sleep when Jack's voice roused me.

"I'm awake, Jack," I said, turning to him.

"Thank goodness," said Jack in English.

"How long have you been up, Jack?"

"I've only just come to and found you here," he replied.

"The ship feels like it's moving," I remarked. "Oh, congratulations on your wonderful gift of speech, Jack. It's an incredible thing! I never suspected you could speak in English way back when. How long have you known?"

"I have long felt that I would speak one day," said Jack, looking bashful. "I never dreamed you could, though I always felt a kinship with you. Somehow the words were always in me, but I guess it took an emergency to get them out."

"It may be even more of an emergency than you know," I

said. "The leader told me that when we reach the open sea they are going to weight down the bodies of the elders and toss them overboard! Somehow, we've got to prevent this."

"Then we will have to escape," said Jack matter-of-factly.

"Yes," I agreed. "Let's see if we can bite each other loose. They were foolish not to gag us."

Jack set to work gnawing at my bonds. His sharp teeth soon cut the twine the poachers had tied us with.

"Good work, Jack," I said, standing and stretching my legs. "Now let's see what I can do for you."

With my legs free, I was able to use my hooves as well as my teeth. I soon had Jack's ropes loosened enough so that he could wriggle out of them.

"Now what?" he asked.

I confess that I was at a loss as to how to answer him. Even with our legs free, we were still locked inside that ship's cabin.

There was nothing to do but wait for a guard to come in the hope that when he opened the door, we could escape. We squatted together on the wooden floor. I grew increasingly anxious with each passing second. The thought that my mother and father might soon be dead deep in the ocean while I sat by helpless tortured me. I began to pace desperately up and down the room, ignoring Jack's pleas that I calm down. Finally, overwhelmed with frustration, I kicked out at the door with my hind legs. I gasped in astonishment when it flew easily open, hit the wall, and swung shut again. Jack and I looked at each other, amazement mirrored on our faces.

"What fools we've been, Jack!" I exclaimed. "The door was

open all along! Johnson must not have relocked it when he came in for his drink before. Let's make haste, Jack, and pray that our good fortune continues." With these words, I pushed the door open again, gently. We stepped out into the hallway. Cautiously we slipped along the corridor until we reached a flight of stairs. Up these we crept. Reaching the top, we stealthily moved onto the ship's deck.

The sunlight made it impossible to see for a moment. As our eyes grew accustomed to light, we saw the entrance to another cabin directly in front of us. Then we heard the sound of footsteps on the stairs we had just ascended. Jack and I hastily hid ourselves behind some nearby barrels.

It was Johnson, the one-eyed poacher, who plodded onto the deck. He opened the door to the cabin and stepped inside. I crept to the doorway and listened to the muffled voices within.

". . . not far enough out yet," said a voice I recognized as that of Walsh, the bald man with the whip who was the leader of the poachers.

"There's no sense putting it off, Walsh; let's get it over with as soon as we can," said Johnson.

Walsh sighed. "Okay then. Just make sure you do the job right. I don't want any live warthogs being picked up!"

I quickly made my way back to Jack Ham.

"They are planning to toss them overboard now, Jack! We've got to stop them!" I whispered urgently.

The cabin door opened, and Johnson stepped out. He walked back down the stairs. Jack and I waited anxiously, our eyes glued to the head of the stairs. A few minutes later four poachers struggled up, hauling a net full of warthogs between them. There were seven or eight elders trapped inside. My heart leapt in fury as I saw my mother among the bunch, the meshes of the net biting painfully into her flesh.

Johnson followed these men. He held a handful of long knives which he gave to the poachers.

"All right," he said, "Walsh is worried about live bodies being recovered. I don't see how they could be, once we ball and chain these devils. But to be on the safe side, let's slit their throats first. You boys won't have a problem doing that, will you?"

The four brutes grinned in a way that turned my blood cold. I was about to rush forward and attack when Jack Ham pawed my shoulder.

"Listen," he whispered.

At first I heard nothing. Soon a low, humming sound became audible. I strained my eyes in the direction of the noise. In the distance, I saw a small dot making its way toward us.

Perhaps help was on the way! I turned my attention back to the poachers. They appeared not to hear the approaching boat, for a human's hearing is not as acute as a warthog's.

One of the men was cutting open the net. I knew something had to be done in the next few seconds. I whispered a few instructions to Jack Ham, then jumped from behind my barrel screaming, "Stop!"

The poachers spun about in shock. Then they lunged at me with their knives. I felt a sharp pain as a blade nicked my ear.

Pure fury swept over me. I have always believed in peace and love, but in some situations, one has to fight. This was such a case. I lowered my head and charged straight into a fat poacher, gouging his legs with my tusks. He cried out, and I ran at another poacher, biting, mauling, and chewing viciously. I even believe a low growl or two escaped from my throat!

Fight as I did, I was still overcome by the sheer force of numbers. Three poachers soon sat on me, holding knives at my head.

Johnson, who had joined in the fight and whose face was now torn and bloody, glared at me in rage.

"Talking warthog or not," he said, "you will die for what you've done. I'm gonna . . ." He stopped speaking suddenly and became alert. He had heard the humming, which was quite loud by now. Johnson ran to the ship's railing and looked in the direction of the noise. Looking after him, I saw a large motorboat rapidly shooting toward us.

The men who held me down sighted the boat also. They climbed off me and ran to Johnson's side. As I got to my feet, I felt our ship grinding to a halt. I smiled to myself, for I knew it was the work of Jack Ham. He had followed my instructions.

The door of Walsh's cabin flew open, and out came Walsh himself. He fled down the stairs but returned moments later, looking crushed. Thirty or forty angry young warthogs, fuming and grunting heatedly, pursued him. Led by Jack Ham, who carried a cleaver between clenched teeth, they were a frightening sight. Many of the other warthogs also carried knives or cleavers.

Jack dropped his weapon on the deck. "We got these from the ship's kitchen," he said.

"Splendid, Jack," I said. "While your group rounds up the rest of the poachers, I'll use your blade to free the elders."

82

With the blade in my teeth, I hacked through the net. In a short while I had made an opening large enough for a warthog to squeeze through. One by one the elders passed through the hole. I was deeply moved to see my mother standing before me, alive and unharmed. Tears of joy welled in my eyes as I kissed her.

The motorboat had pulled up at our ship's side. Troy and Adam jumped onto the deck, followed by a black man in a police uniform, whom they introduced as Captain Lewcey.

"Hey," I called to them, "you're just in time. Here comes Jack Ham's group now." As I spoke the young warthogs were marching a group of poachers to the center of the deck.

Captain Lewcey's men quickly came aboard and began handcuffing the poachers. It was a wonderful sight.

"Wart!" cried Adam. "Thank heavens you're okay! As soon as we came to, we went to the local police. Captain Lewcey told us he suspected the Walsh gang, who specialize in capturing exceptional animals to sell stateside. The bums! But they'll get theirs."

"I must commend you on your excellent timing," I said. "Five minutes more and I would not be standing here."

"We found the harbor that you left from," said Troy. "Then we used radar to track down the poachers' ship. It was child's play."

Soon all the warthogs on the ship had been freed. I stood and surveyed the crowd. I saw Horgor and his group, the lovely Jasmeena, and others. Old Zareemba trotted over to me.

"I am proud of you," he said in Warthog. "You have saved

the entire tribe. You have always been exceptional, even though you suffered greatly for it. I am old now, and will die soon. Will you stay with us and lead the tribe?"

I said nothing for several moments. Again, I looked at my tribe. I studied the faces that had taunted me so short a while ago and caught Jasmeena's eye.

"Please accept," she said.

"Yes," said someone else. "Lead us!"

One by one the members of the tribe began to shout their encouragement. Even Horgor raised his voice, begging me to stay.

Once I would have given everything for a moment like this. But now it didn't seem so important. I was outgrowing the old longing to be like the others. Besides, I knew my destiny was elsewhere. I looked at Jack Ham and knew what I must say.

I laughed, trying to sound lighthearted. "I have just turned down kingship of a human country, honored Zareemba. Your offer is tempting, but my place is with my friends, Troy and Adam. I think you will find another exceptional warthog in Jack Ham. Jack should be your successor—he will bring great strength and wisdom to the tribe." I met Jack's eyes and smiled. "After all, it was he who shut down the ship's engine and freed the young warthogs. Jack Ham is the hero of the day!"

7

A New Life

Two days later I stood in the blazing sun near the jungle at the edge of the African airport. With me were Troy, Adam, Christopher, my parents, and Jack Ham. Alhazred, our pilot, was waiting for us. We had left the village that morning, after spending a couple of days helping to reconstruct it. The Walsh gang had left it pretty much a shambles. Our plane was ready to take off, and I was glad to be going back to America.

Christopher strained at the leash with which Alhazred had secured him. He seemed to be watching something in the trees.

"I wonder what's making him so nervous?" asked Adam. "Let's see what the story is." Adam removed the leash from Christopher's neck. The monkey was off in a flash with us hurrying behind him.

"Look there," said Troy, pointing.

High up on a branch, Christopher sat next to a female monkey who grabbed his hand. They gibbered back and forth excitedly.

"Get a load of that," laughed Adam. "Looks like old Christopher has found himself a girlfriend! What do you think, Wart?"

"I'd say it was the call of nature, Adam, and there's no use trying to interfere."

We watched Christopher and his lady friend as they swung into another tree. The monkey seemed to look back and wink at us. Then they both vanished into the jungle.

The group of us turned back to the airstrip where Alhazred stood. "You know, I'll miss Christopher," said Troy. "But I guess it's all for the best. He was born to live wild."

Before bidding farewell to Africa, I took a last look around. I felt that I would return someday to see how Jack Ham made out as the tribe's leader. I kissed my mother and father goodbye and wished Jack luck. Moments later, the boys and I were in the air, headed toward New York.

We arrived at Kennedy Airport on a cool March morning. The year was 1966. As we got off the plane, all three of us were grinning from ear to ear.

Alhazred, whom we had become friendly with during our trip, surprised us by giving us a small trunk. It had been sent along by King Hasaami, he told us, as a gift. The trunk contained a small fortune in jewels. We also received an envelope containing a nice sum of American currency. We thanked Alhazred heartily and told him to send our best wishes to King Hasaami.

"May good luck be with you always," he said, as he prepared to leave us.

"And with you," the three of us said as one. We strolled off to find a taxi.

During the ride we spoke animatedly of all that had happened since we had first left New York. We decided to split the money and jewels evenly.

"This will be a nice nest egg to send us through college, Adam," said Troy.

"I suppose so," said Adam. "Right now I need some new clothes, and I've been wanting to buy an electric guitar for a while. And I want to get something nice for Janie. I guess if there's anything left over, maybe I'll bank it."

"A fool and his money are soon parted," said Troy, looking disapprovingly at his brother. "Say, Wart, what'll you do with your share?"

I thought for a moment. "I think I'll let you hold it for me, Troy," I said, "and if I need it, I'll ask you." I was remembering my surprise mud bath last Christmas and was thinking of what I'd buy for the boys the next year.

"That's wise," nodded Troy. "But what will we tell my aunt?"

"The simplest thing is to tell the truth," I said.

"*That's* simple?" asked Adam. "Brother! She'll probably put us in the loony bin! But you're right, Wart. Honesty is the best policy, and all that stuff. What do you say, Troy?"

"I think Wart's right, too," said Troy. "You guys know Aunt Amarantha isn't all that sharp, and she'll probably be so happy to see us that she'll believe anything. I'm worried about the FBI, though. They'll be angry that we boarded the rocket and then let it crash."

"I'll handle that," said Adam with a mysterious smile. After that, he didn't say another word for the rest of the ride.

We reached Aunt Aramantha's and Troy paid the driver, tipping him with one of the jewels Hasaami had given us. The fellow turned white as he stared at it with bulging eyes. He was speechless. We unloaded our trunk and left him standing.

We took the elevator to Aunt Aramantha's floor. "Well, here goes nothing," said Adam, and rang the bell.

Aramantha Armstrong answered presently. When she saw the boys, she burst into tears and threw her arms around them.

"Oh, boys, it's good to see you!" she cried. "I thought you were dead until I received your cable! Dr. Fredericks told me you'd been flung into outer space or some such rot."

When he could free himself from her embrace, Adam introduced me as "a close friend." Aunt Aramantha looked at me strangely for a moment. I gave her a friendly greeting and a broad smile. Then, wiping the tears from her eyes, she ushered us all inside. We made ourselves comfortable in the living room, and Aunt Aramantha began to bombard the boys with questions.

"One moment," said Troy, laughing. "Maybe if we tell you the entire story, it'll save time."

Everyone agreed, and Troy told the strange tale of our trip to Phobos and our adventures in Karobia and Africa. He told his aunt almost everything, except that I had lived in her home for several months without her noticing me.

Aunt Aramantha sat engrossed in Troy's narrative. When he had finished, she looked at him with amusement.

"Boys," she said, her wrinkled face beaming, "I've a good

mind to wear both your hides out! Imagine, staying away all this time without a word except a telegram. And then to show up with a wild tale like that! If you weren't so big, I'd spank you both! And you, too, War-Tug, or whatever your name is!"

"But . . ." began Troy.

"And you have quite an imagination, Troy. Such talk about giant bees and princes and poachers! I don't know where you picked up that creature and that trunk, and I don't care. Now I'll get dinner started. Don't run off again!" With that, she toddled off into the kitchen. As she left I heard her mumbling, "Boys will be boys!"

Troy, Adam, and I all looked at one another. We burst out laughing hysterically.

"She hasn't believed a word of our story!" said Adam.

"Perhaps it is best this way," I said, "for now nothing much will be made of our trip to Phobos."

"Let's hope not," said Troy. "I still suspect the U.S. government might be curious about its rocket. It worries me."

"I told you guys," said Adam, looking smug. "We've got nothing to worry about. Leave it to me."

Troy looked at his brother curiously. "That's just what I'm worried about," he said.

At this point Aunt Aramantha returned with a plate of cookies and glasses of milk, which we eagerly accepted.

"I shouldn't let you spoil your dinner this way, but this is a special occasion. You boys had best tidy up with hot showers and a change of clothes. Your—er—friend can wait in your room."

A half hour later all three of us sat at the dining room table, which was filled with delicious-looking vegetables and fruits. There was a large roast ham there, too, but this I naturally disregarded. We also ate steaming hot biscuits, and we had ginger ale to drink. Dessert consisted of a tapioca pudding topped with whipped cream.

At the end of that wonderful meal, I felt bloated and sleepy. We excused ourselves and went into the boys' bedroom.

That night Adam made a few phone calls from the living room. He told us to be up early for an important appointment, but would tell us no more.

The next morning we left the house early and took a cab to the high school the boys attended. In front of the building Adam introduced Troy and me to a Dr. Milton Roddenberg, a thin, sharp-eyed young man in his mid-twenties. Mr. Roddenberg was dressed in a colorful silk suit and had hair even longer than Adam's.

"Mr. Roddenberg is a lawyer," said Adam. "I met him at a show by the Byrds last year. He's going to help us talk to Dr. Fredericks."

The four of us entered the school building. Dr. Fredericks's office was on the second floor, and we found him sitting at his desk, talking with two serious-looking men wearing brown suits and sunglasses.

Troy spoke first. "Hello, Dr. Fredericks."

"Hello, Troy," answered his teacher. "It's wonderful to see you again! For a while we'd given you up for dead! Then your aunt called about your telegram. What happened?"

"It's a long story," said Adam, eyeing the men in brown. "Mr.

Roddenberg will be speaking for us today, sir. We are all still very disturbed from our trip."

"I should imagine," said Dr. Fredericks, sizing up Milton Roddenberg, who stood quietly behind us. "You might be wondering who these two men are, boys. This is . . ."

The fellow at the right of the desk stepped forward quickly and pulled out his wallet.

"Jack Tucker, FBI," he said, flashing his badge.

The other man in brown showed his badge. "Bill Gallagher, CIA," he said.

Dr. Fredericks cleared his throat. "As unpleasant as it may seem, boys, Mr. Tucker and Mr. Gallagher need to speak to you and that, uh, warthog of yours. The government is very upset."

Milton Roddenberg spoke suddenly. Pulling out his wallet, he handed both Tucker and Gallagher one of his business cards.

"I'm so glad you gentlemen are here," he said. "This little meeting can save the government a lot of embarrassment. I really hate to think of what would happen if the papers heard about the boys' experience."

"What do you mean?" asked Jack Tucker, examining the lawyer's card.

"I mean," said Mr. Roddenberg, drawing himself up to his full height, which was well over six feet, "that these two boys and their friend have suffered greatly at the hands of a bunch of trained goons. To be chased onto a rocket ship and shot into space to who knows where! These boys are lucky to be alive now. No thanks to Uncle Sam, I'm sorry to say." He shook his head, looking tired.

Tucker and Gallagher exchanged worried looks.

Before either could speak, Milton Roddenberg plunged on.

"Of course, my clients do not wish to see this business in the newspapers. Nor do they wish to take their case to court. They would be happy if they were just left in peace."

"Wait a second, here," began Bill Gallagher, whose face had turned a deep shade of red.

Mr. Roddenberg went on as though he hadn't heard him.

"If the thing did go to court," he said, smiling pleasantly, "I don't know how many careers would be needlessly ruined." He glanced sharply at Gallagher, whose face had changed rapidly from red to white.

"Of course," continued our lawyer, "my clients would just as soon forget anything ever happened. As, I am certain, you gentlemen would also. Am I correct?"

After a few seconds, Tucker and Gallagher nodded.

"I'm so glad we all understand one another," said Milton Roddenberg. "Please call if you have any questions. Good day, gentlemen." He turned and left. Adam, Troy, and I followed.

In front of the school, the boys shook hands with Mr. Roddenberg, who cheerfully told Adam there would be no fee for his services.

"That was for the pure enjoyment of it," he told us before hopping into his Volkswagon, which was parked nearby.

During the subway ride home, Troy was sullen.

"What's wrong?" asked Adam.

"I hope that Dr. Fredericks doesn't get in trouble because of us," said Troy. "He's helped me a lot."

"Don't worry," said Adam. "I filled him in on everything last night. He knew Mr. Roddenberg was coming. But I think we've heard the last from Mr. FBI and Mr. CIA. Did you see how they looked when Milton said their careers might be in danger? They won't bother Dr. Fredericks or us."

Troy looked at his brother and permitted himself a small smile. "I've got to admit it was clever," he chuckled. "You know, Adam, when you take your mind off girls and rock 'n' roll for a moment, you're not so dumb."

The following few months went by quickly. We didn't get out much, for the boys were busy catching up on their schoolwork. Aunt Aramantha reluctantly accepted me as a member of the household, which meant that I had to share the chores. I was happy to do this. For example, the boys helped me to attach scrub brushes to my front hooves. I took a few falls on soapy floors, but eventually got the hang of it. It was good to feel I was pulling my own weight.

When the boys were busy, I'd sometimes go out on my own. Though I still attracted a lot of stares, I was much more confident than I had ever been. I would hail cabs and order food from restaurants without the least problem. Adam often said that New Yorkers weren't shocked by anything and, perhaps because I no longer minded being different, I was treated like any other citizen.

Time passed, and summer vacation rolled around. I began to get restless. Troy spent his free time working on a science project which he hoped would win him a scholarship. Adam spent his first few weeks off dating girls and going to rock shows.

One morning Adam announced that he was going to look for a summer job.

"A miracle," said Troy. "The poet wants to work."

Adam ignored this. "Would you like to come along with me, Wart? Maybe we can find something for you, too."

I replied that I'd be delighted to accompany him. I dressed in a summer suit and put on a warthog-sized homburg hat. Adam kept on his uniform of blue jeans and sneakers, but did put on a white button-down shirt rather than his usual T-shirt.

We left the house with no idea of where we were going. It was a fine, clear day, and both Adam and I were in high spirits. We began walking downtown. At around twelve o'clock we reached that section of the city known as Greenwich Village. We found ourselves on a street of small stores. Gaily dressed people walked by all around us, paying me no heed.

Suddenly Adam let out a happy cry.

"What is it?" I asked.

"Look there!" he said, pointing in the direction of a shop. "It looks like just what the doctor ordered!"

It was a little shop with the words "SANFORD'S PIZZERIA" stencilled on the window. Below this a hand-lettered sign was propped up. It read: "HELP WANTED. FREE ROOM AND BOARD. APPLY INSIDE."

"Employment *and* lodging?" I said. "Let's check this out."

"Okey-doke," said Adam, stepping briskly ahead of me. I followed him as he entered the pizzeria. We were greeted by the aroma of freshly baked pies. A round, short man with a big black beard regarded us from behind the counter.

94

"May I help you?" he asked.

"We saw your sign in the window," said Adam. " 'Help wanted.' "

"Ah!" said the bearded man. "Wonderful. I just put out the sign a little while ago. As a matter of fact, I just opened the place a couple of weeks ago. Business has been so good that I find I can't get along without help. Sit down and let's talk. My name is Sanford Da Capo."

Adam introduced himself, and I explained who I was, saying that for personal reasons, I was known to my friends as "Wart."

"To be honest with you," said Sanford, leaning against the counter, "the job pays very little. But, as my sign says, you will have a place to stay and you'll be well fed. You are to help me make and sell my pizza pies—which are delicious, may I add— and attend to little things in the shop."

Adam explained to Mr. Da Capo that he would be returning to school in September and really only wanted a summer job.

"Hmmm," said Sanford, stroking his beard. "I really wanted someone permanent. But I like your face, Adam. I need help, so you can start at noon. I don't know about your—uh—friend. The Board of Health might object to an animal on the premises."

"Wart's one of the cleanest individuals around!" said Adam indignantly.

"Well, that may be, but I'm not sure I can hire him. Don't get me wrong, but . . .'"

"If I can't work here with Wart, then this is the wrong job for me," said Adam sadly. "It's too bad that some people won't give another creature a chance just because he's different."

"Hold on a second," replied Sanford. He studied me closely. I gave him my most winning smile.

"Well, Wart *does* seem to give off a positive vibration, and I usually judge people—that is, individuals—by my feelings. Maybe customers would enjoy having a warthog waiting tables. Okay, fellows—you're both hired!"

Adam and I looked at each other and nodded. "Thank you, sir," said Adam.

"Good. But none of that 'sir' stuff. It's Sanford." He looked at me thoughtfully. "We'll work it this way: Adam will help me make the pies and cut them into slices. The Warthog here will deliver them to the tables. We can strap a tray on his back. People can leave their money on the tray after getting their pizza, and he can bring back change."

"Very clever," I commented. Sanford shrugged off the compliment with a smile.

At this point Adam asked Sanford if he would excuse us for a moment. We stepped outside the shop.

"It looks like luck was with us," Adam said. "The thing I wanted to ask you, Wart, was this: Although you've gotten comfortable at Aunt Aramantha's place, I would like to take advantage of the free living quarters that go with the job. I think it would be a good experience to be on my own for a couple of months. How do you feel about coming, too?"

"Adam," I said, "I think a change of pace would do me good as well. I'd like to stay with you."

"Great!" said Adam, clapping me on the back.

We went back into the pizzeria. It was getting near noon, and

Sanford briefed us on our duties. He fastened a large metal tray to my back, tying it under my belly with an elastic strap. At five minutes to twelve, he removed a lot of steaming hot pies from the oven and handed Adam a pizza cutter.

"In the short time I've been open, word has gotten around that my pizza is the best in the city. Business is brisk, and we get a lot of interesting customers. Watch."

He opened the door to the shop. Already a line of people waited outside. They began to file in. Many were on a first-name basis with Sanford. Quite an assortment they were, too: businessmen and hippies, secretaries and poets, factory workers and bookshop clerks.

It was a hectic first day, and we were on the move until six o'clock, when the night staff arrived. I was exhausted, and I could tell by looking at Adam that he was, too.

Sanford congratulated us and said he thought we'd work out fine. He showed us to our living quarters, a comfortable room at the rear of the shop. It contained a bunk bed, a desk, and two chairs. He told us to make ourselves at home.

Adam and I playfully tossed a coin to decide who was to sleep where. As it turned out, I got the lower bunk, which made the most sense, anyway. We decided we'd wake up early the next morning and get our things from Aunt Aramantha's.

Aunt Aramantha made a fuss when Adam told her what we'd done. But my friend could be very charming when the need arose, and he reminded her it was only for the summer. In the end, she said she thought it was good that Adam would be earning his own money.

"After all," she said, "it's a positive sign that you've got some ambitions in life other than chasing girls and listening to that sock-hop and roll noise all the time."

"It's rock 'n' roll, Aunt Aramantha," said Adam.

"Well, whatever it is, anything that wild and loud can't be good for a young man. It would certainly never help you earn a living, and the sooner you outgrow it, the better."

When we related our news to Troy, he told Adam that we'd both "flipped a gear," but he said he'd come visit us and sample the pizza.

So we moved into Sanford's Pizzeria. For six hours a day we worked hard. At night Adam and I were tired. Still, we had much to talk about because we were daily exposed to a great number of interesting people. It was a new life for me.

8

The Missing Emerald

One morning, before the shop opened for business, there was a rapping at the glass door. I glanced up from the table where Adam and I were talking. Adam's back was to the door, and over his shoulder I could see the figure of Troy Armstrong grinning in the doorway.

Adam turned. "Troy's here!" he shouted. He bounded out of his chair and let his brother in.

"Troy!" he said, hugging him. "I never thought I'd say it, but I've missed you. It's good to see you!"

"You, too," Troy said, clapping Adam on the shoulder. "And how are you, Wart?"

I replied that I was very well. Adam went behind the counter to brew some coffee, and Troy sat down at a table with me.

We talked for a while. Troy told me that his science project was near completion. It was something to do with molecular reconstruction, but when he started to describe it, I stopped him.

"It's a bit over my head," I said, laughing. He looked very well, I thought. He was dressed quite casually in chino pants, sneakers, and a striped shirt.

Sanford came out from his back room to see what the commotion was. I introduced them.

"Any brother of Adam's and friend of the Warthog's is a brother and friend to me," said Sanford.

Adam returned with coffee, and the four of us sat and chatted. Troy, it turned out, had been in the area picking up some supplies for his project from a nearby warehouse. He had brought the daily newspaper in with him, and my eye chanced to fall on the cover story. Skimming over the article, I noticed a familiar name.

"Look at this," I said, speaking to Sanford. "Tom is on a case."

Officer Thomas O'Riley was a police detective who ate lunch regularly at the pizzeria. I read the article out loud. It stated that the Peridome Emerald, a stone of untold value owned by millionaire Jim Shoes III, had been stolen the night before from Mr. Shoes's suite in the Hotel Le Beaux. The theft was being investigated by Detective O'Riley.

"Say, that's something," said Adam. "I guess we'll hear the whole story at lunchtime."

At about a quarter to twelve, fifteen minutes before we usually opened, there was another rapping at the door. This time it was Officer O'Riley.

Tom O'Riley was a big, middle-aged man with a kindly face

and flecks of gray in his hair. He was usually jovial and talkative, but today his face was pinched and his eyes puffy. He looked as though he had stayed up all night worrying.

"Good morning," said the policeman. "I know you're not open yet, but I need a cup of coffee badly. May I come in?"

"Of course, Tom," said Sanford amiably, gesturing for him to enter. O'Riley hurried in and pulled a chair up to our table. Adam poured him a cup of coffee, and I introduced Troy to the detective. O'Riley barely acknowledged him. He looked lost in his own thoughts.

"What's the matter, Tom?" I asked him directly.

"Haven't you heard, Mr. Warthog?" he said. "The Peridome Emerald has been stolen, and I've been assigned to the case."

"You've solved many another case," I pointed out. "Does this one present special problems?"

O'Riley groaned. "It sure does," he said. "Old man Shoes is very unpleasant and uncooperative. He's in a bad mood about this emerald, and he's threatened to get me fired if I don't recover the stone. With his power and influence, he can do it. On top of that, I can't find any clues at all."

"You've found *nothing* to go on?" asked Troy.

"Nothing," answered O'Riley glumly.

"Come now," I said. "Tell us the facts as you see them."

"Okay," he said. "It goes like this. Jim Shoes III checked into the Hotel Le Beaux several days ago. He brought along the Peridome Emerald, for some reason which he won't tell me.

"The stone was discovered to be missing last night. Shoes got out of bed at approximately 1 A.M., for he has trouble sleeping.

Something made him open his jewel case. He found the emerald gone. He immediately phoned the police, and they put me on the job. I've been up all night looking for clues. Nothing!"

"No fingerprints?" asked Adam.

"None," said O'Riley.

"Could it have been an inside job?" asked Sanford.

"Yeah, maybe the butler did it," said Adam. Everyone looked at him with disgust.

"No," said Tom O'Riley. "Everyone on the hotel staff was given lie detector tests. No luck."

"Sounds like a tough case, all right," said Sanford. "I'd like to talk more, but we've got to open up soon."

"Yes," said O'Riley, "I've got to get going myself. No time for lunch today." He rose to go.

"Wait a bit, Tom," I said. "Sometimes an outside opinion can be helpful. Maybe if Adam, Troy, and I worked with you, we could turn something up. Perhaps later tonight?"

He appeared to consider this. "It's highly irregular," he said. "But from the stories you've told me, Warthog, you and the boys have come through some strange things with flying colors. Maybe you'll bring me luck. All right, then, you can come along. How about you, Sanford?"

The bearded man shook his head. "Count me out. I'm allergic to danger."

"Okay, I'll pick you three up out front at six-thirty this evening. See you later." With those words, he left, opening the door for our first group of customers.

That day went by very slowly, but at last it was over. Troy

went back home and then met us outside the pizzeria at the appointed time. O'Riley picked us up in a squad car and brought us to the hotel. As we walked across the lobby, a thin, nervous-looking fellow ran over to us.

"Officer! Mr. Shoes has threatened to sue the hotel! What shall I do?"

"Take it easy," said O'Riley brusquely, stepping past the man, who looked like a frightened rabbit. "I'll handle it." Troy, Adam, and I followed him into the waiting elevator.

"That was Grafton Pendleton, the hotel manager," said O'Riley. "You see how Shoes affects people?"

The elevator ascended quickly and opened on the penthouse floor. We walked down a richly carpeted hallway. At the far end was a large oak door with an armed police officer before it. At a word from O'Riley, he stepped aside and opened the door for us. We entered the luxury suite of Jim Shoes III.

From out of a room that we could not see came a harsh voice. "Who's there?" it bellowed. "Who could get past my guard?"

"It's Officer O'Riley, sir, and some friends," said Tom.

A few seconds later, a tiny man came bustling into the room where we stood. Jim Shoes III was not much more than five feet tall. He was dressed in silk pajamas and a scarlet smoking jacket. He had the air of a man used to being obeyed.

He looked at our group. "What is this? A party?" he asked. Before O'Riley could reply, Shoes addressed him in a nasty tone. "Haven't you bungled this case enough already? How come you're not out searching for the thief? And what is *that* doing in my hotel suite?" He pointed a finger at me.

"*That* is a friend of mine, Mr. Warthog by name," said O'Riley, looking rather flustered. "He is here to help on the case."

Shoes laughed unpleasantly. "Do you really think I am going to permit this beast to go nosing in my affairs? I should say not! Officer, take this misshapen bloodhound from my chambers!"

"Pardon me," I said, just managing to keep my tone civil. "But I have Officer O'Riley's authority to ask you a few questions. We all hope they'll help to uncomplicate this sticky matter."

The millionaire glared at me. "A talking warthog! I guess you fancy yourself quite clever, huh? Well, let me warn you: I have no liking for your kind. On my last safari in Africa, a warthog attacked me! Savage beasts!"

"It's a good thing that the human race is not judged by the behavior of one individual," I responded. "If I had met you before I met my friends here, I would have thought all mankind to be rude, cruel, and angry."

Shoes flushed a deep red but said nothing. After a moment he mumbled, "I'm sorry."

"Quite all right," I said. "Now I have some questions for you. Why did you bring the Peridome Emerald here to the hotel?"

"It's a personal matter," said Shoes. "I told O'Riley that already. I didn't want any information leaking out to the papers. But if you must know, I brought it as a gift to the woman I wish to marry."

"Her name?" I queried.

"See here! There's no reason to drag her into this. She was not even supposed to know I was in town. It was to be a surprise!"

"Mr. Shoes, you didn't tell me this," broke in Tom O'Riley. "What else are you holding back?"

"Nothing," said Shoes, stubbornly.

"What is your fiancée's name, Mr. Shoes?" I persisted.

"Very well. Her name is Jennifer Wood. But I do not want you disturbing her with this."

"We'll see," said O'Riley.

"I understand that the hotel staff has been questioned," I continued. "Did you bring any personal servants along with you?"

Shoes nodded. "I did. Miss Leslie North has been my personal maid for the past nine years. Her loyalty is beyond question."

"Does she have access to your things?" I pressed on.

"Of course. But she would never think of stealing. I pay her well. She's a fine woman. Why, when I told her the Peridome Emerald was gone, she fainted dead away. She's been resting today. I didn't mention her before because I didn't want the poor dear disturbed."

Tom O'Riley slapped his forehead with his palm. "Mr. Shoes, I wish you'd told me this before! Where is the lady now?"

"She's in her room on the third floor. She is not to be disturbed, though. Doctor's orders," said Shoes.

"She'll probably have to be questioned later," stated O'Riley.

I had asked all the questions I wanted to. Adam, Troy, and I bid farewell to Mr. Shoes and rode down to the lobby, where we waited for Officer O'Riley. I explained my theory about the case to the boys, and they both nodded excitedly at the plan I outlined.

A few minutes later, O'Riley joined us.

"Well, Mr. Warthog," he said, "What do you think?"

"I think that one of these two women holds the key to this theft," I replied.

"Exactly what I was thinking!" said O'Riley proudly. "I got the address of Shoes's girlfriend, Miss Jennifer Wood. I'll question her tonight. Tomorrow I'll talk to the maid. Mr. Warthog, I can't thank you enough for getting that information out of Shoes. He was tight as a clam this morning."

"It was nothing," I said. "But the boys and I were thinking, Tom. We'd like to hang around and do some window shopping. Also, we can keep an eye out for any suspicious characters."

O'Riley looked amused. "Suit yourselves," he said. "But I think I'll be wrapping up the case very nicely in a day or so." Whistling happily, he got into the squad car and drove off.

"How do you like that?" chuckled Adam. "There's gratitude for you."

"That's all right," I said. "If our plan works, he'll whistle a different tune. He's a good man, though, and he will get the credit if things work out the way I think they will."

"And if they don't, no one will be the wiser," said Troy. "Wart, you're growing by leaps and bounds! A year ago you would never have been able to take charge like this."

It was true. I hadn't thought about it, but the actions I had taken had been instinctive. And, more importantly, they had felt correct.

"Well," I said. "Let's put our plan into effect. Troy, we'll need some stationery, an envelope, and a pen. Other than that, a little luck will do. Let's go!"

Twenty minutes later Adam and I sat in the hotel lobby awaiting the bellboy we had sent to Miss North's room. Troy was around the corner in a coffee shop. He had brought us what we needed and was waiting for us to complete our plan.

"Now we'll see how well our gambit worked," I whispered to Adam as the boy approached us.

"Miss North says she will see you now," he said.

We thanked him and rode the elevator to the third floor. At room 305 we stopped, and Adam knocked sharply on the door.

"Glenn!" came an urgent female voice from within. "Come in before it's too late! We can still . . . say, wait a minute! You're not Glenn!"

Adam and I had stepped into the room and now stood looking at Jim Shoes III's maid. She was a pretty woman of about thirty with long brown hair. There were large circles under her eyes, which were red from unshed tears.

"The game is over, Miss North," I said slowly. "Why don't you tell us about it?"

"You—you know about Glenn and me?" she asked.

"I can guess. If you will just begin at the beginning," I said gently.

Miss North began to cry. She sat down on the edge of her bed and, between tears and choking sobs, told us the following story.

"I was such a fool! And I deserve whatever happens. That smooth-talking man! You see, it was on our first day in New York that it happened. Mr. Shoes let me have the day off to go sightseeing. At the Empire State Building a handsome, polite man approached me. He introduced himself as Mr. Glenn Cornick. We began to talk.

"He was so charming that I began to tell him about myself. I told him I was personal maid to the famous Jim Shoes III. He claimed to be interested in the history of the Peridome Emerald, which he knew Mr. Shoes owned. I let it slip that Mr. Shoes had brought it with him. I should have seen then what he was up to, when he started asking me where Mr. Shoes kept the stone. But I thought he was just interested in me and my work. How could I have been so dumb?

"I made a date to go to dinner with him. Over dinner he told me he loved me. He said he wanted to elope with me. Yesterday at midnight I let him into my room. He said he'd wait for me while I packed. But when I came out with my suitcase, he was gone. Naturally, I was very upset. Later I found my hotel room keys missing. When I heard that the emerald had been stolen, I put two and two together. But I couldn't bring myself to tell Mr. Shoes what I knew. I hoped that Glenn would turn himself in. Then, when I got the letter, I thought . . . Oh, dear!" Here she began to sob hysterically.

"It's all right, Miss North," said Adam kindly. "You've been tricked by a con man. It's not your fault. Well, Sherlock Warthog, what next?"

"Now we notify Tom and find this Glenn Cornick fellow. Let's hope he hasn't already gotten away," I said. "If you'll make the phone call, Adam, I'll look after Miss North."

Adam was able to reach Officer O'Riley through the police dispatcher, who sent the message to his squad car radio. In half

108

an hour O'Riley met us in front of the hotel. Leslie North had given me Glenn Cornick's address, and Troy had already taken a cab there. His instructions were to keep an eye on the building and to wait for us to show up.

Adam and I filled O'Riley in on all we had learned. He seemed very surprised and perhaps a little angry, too. But he drove quickly to Glenn Cornick's address, which was a run-down building on Eleventh Avenue. We met Troy, who was standing against a street lamp on the corner.

"No one has come or gone while I've been here," he said.

The four of us entered the building and rang the superintendent's bell. A man in a sleeveless undershirt answered.

O'Riley flashed his badge. "Police business," he said, explaining we needed to be let into Cornick's apartment.

The super went to fetch a set of keys. "I knew that bum was no good," he mumbled to himself. Shaking his head, he led us up three flights of stairs. He knocked at Cornick's door. When there was no answer, he used one of his keys to open it. The apartment was empty.

"He's flown the coop," said O'Riley in disgust, looking around the dingy and unkempt apartment.

My heart sank. I should have realized that Cornick wouldn't have stayed in New York a moment longer than necessary.

Adam sank down onto the couch. "What a drag," he sighed.

I began to nose into a pile of papers by the telephone. "Look here," I shouted. I held out a scrap of paper in my teeth.

O'Riley took it and read it aloud.

"K. Airport. 10:47 P.M. San Fran."

"That must mean the 10:47 flight to San Francisco at Kennedy Airport," I said.

O'Riley looked at his watch. "It's ten minutes till ten. We can beat him to it if we leave now!"

"Wait a minute," said Adam. "How do we know he didn't leave last night?"

"The crime was committed too late in the evening," I said. "He could not have caught the 10:47 flight last night."

"Then what are we waiting for?" said Troy. "Let's move!"

O'Riley drove like a speed demon. We raced into the main terminal at Kennedy Airport at 10:30. It was the work of but a few moments to find out what airline had a 10:47 flight to San Francisco. By 10:35, we were watching the plane in question.

When the passengers began to board, Adam whispered excitedly. "I'll bet that's him," he said, pointing to a handsome man in a cheap-looking black suit. He wore sunglasses, carried a small bag, and kept looking around nervously.

"I'd stake my badge on it," said O'Riley. The detective moved boldly forward. "You there," he called. "I want a word with . . ."

O'Riley never finished the sentence, for the nervous man ran at him, hitting him on the head with his bag. O'Riley went down, stunned.

Troy and Adam both made a grab at Cornick, but he slipped through their grip and continued running across the airport. My legs sprang into action, and I took up the chase.

Warthogs can run quickly and, though Cornick was fast, I overtook him. I dived at his back, planting my tusks in the seat of his pants. He howled and fell to the ground.

110

Seconds later Troy and Adam, followed by O'Riley, came running up. The boys grabbed Cornick by his arms.

"She squealed on me, did she?" growled Cornick. "I shoulda caught the first flight out of town yesterday! But like a sap I hung around all day, thinking maybe I should take her with me. Dames and crime just don't mix! Darn that broad!"

"That's enough," said Detective Thomas O'Riley, slapping a pair of handcuffs on him. "Where's the stone?"

"In the bag, copper," said Glenn Cornick.

Adam opened the bag and dug through it. He unwrapped a wad of tissue paper and took a glowing stone from within it.

"Mr. Shoes will eat his words, now," said O'Riley, beaming.

The next morning Troy, Adam, and I sat with Officer O'Riley and Sanford at a table in the pizzeria.

"But what made you suspect the maid had been conned?" asked Sanford, who had been listening with interest.

"It was when Mr. Shoes told me she had fainted after he discovered the emerald stolen," I replied. "An extreme reaction, even from a dedicated servant. I suspected she'd been taken in by a con man pretending to be in love with her. I had Troy write a letter asking to see her 'one last time.' He signed it, 'Your one true love.' I knew that we would be able to tell from her reaction if she were involved in any way."

O'Riley chuckled. "Mr. Warthog, I've got a lot to thank you for. Glenn Cornick, I've discovered, has a dozen aliases and is wanted for crimes from here to California. He's usually a smooth operator, but he slipped up this time. We're glad to have him under wraps now!"

There is little more to be told about the case of the Peridome Emerald. Glenn Cornick, of course, wound up in prison. Jim Shoes III married his sweetheart at a glorious wedding to which we were all invited (Sanford's Pizzeria provided the food for the reception). The unfortunate Leslie North was forgiven by her employer. I understand that she finally met a decent young man in advertising and got married herself some time later.

It is also worth mentioning that Officer Thomas O'Riley was promoted. He currently ranks quite high in the police force because of his involvement in the case. O'Riley had wanted me to share in the glory by making me an honorary police detective, but I had refused. I was glad to see O'Riley advance but was content to stay in the background, knowing my worth was appreciated by a few good people.

9

The Fabulous Twins

About two weeks after we solved the case of the Peridome Emerald, Adam and I met two men who would change our lives forever. It was in August 1966, shortly before Adam was to return to school.

While we were working at Sanford's, we met a great many fascinating people. But none were so strange and marvelous as Edwin and Peter Cambricke, the Fabulous Twins.

We first met them on a Monday morning at about 11 A.M. Sanford had started opening the pizzeria early for breakfast. That morning the shop was empty; it was too late for breakfast and not quite time for lunch. Adam and I were resting at one of the tables when two of the oddest-looking characters I had ever seen walked in.

They each stood a good six-foot-four, but they seemed much taller because they both wore foot-high top hats. They had to bend over to get through the door. Their thin bodies moved almost in unison as they walked toward us.

The twins were dressed in white silk suits, pink shirts, and black ties. One of them alone would have been a sight; the two of them, identical in every way, were startling to look at.

"Good morning," they said together, tipping their hats to Adam and me with friendly smiles. They were both completely bald. I noticed a trace of an accent in their speech. "We would like two cups of tea, if it would be no trouble." I identified the accent as British and smiled. Ever since I read Dickens back in the cabin in the bush, I'd had a special love for British things.

"No trouble at all," I said. "Please have a seat. We like our customers to be comfortable."

"A good policy," said one of the twins, smiling.

Adam fixed two cups of tea and brought them to the table. As they sipped, the twins stared at me curiously with steel gray eyes.

"Pardon me," said one, "but you are a talking warthog, are you not?"

"Yes, indeed," I said proudly. "We're a very rare breed."

"That's true," said Adam. "My buddy Wart is a real special little guy. We've had some pretty wild adventures together, too."

"They have not ended yet," said one of the twins mysteriously. "But come, you gentlemen must have names. Ours are Edwin and Peter Cambricke—I'm Edwin, he's Peter—and, as I suppose you can see, we are identical twins."

Adam and I introduced ourselves, and I explained to the twins my reasons for remaining nameless since my youth. To change the subject I asked the twins what they did for a living.

"We are magicians," said one (I think now it was Peter, though at the time I could not tell them apart). "We go under the name of 'The Fabulous Twins.'"

"You're professionals, then?" asked Adam.

"Of course!" said one, almost indignantly. "We have lived with magic all our lives."

"Is it not true that what is called magic is really ninety-nine percent showmanship?" I asked. "Illusions and tricks played on the audience?"

"Tricks? Illusion?" answered a twin. "My dear fellow, if you doubt the power of magic, let us show you that it works." He took a thin tube, about a foot long, from his jacket pocket.

"A magic wand?" asked Adam, amused.

"Quite so," said the twin with the wand. "Now, watch closely." He pointed his wand at his now empty teacup. Squinting as if deep in thought, he muttered some words. As we watched, the cup disappeared without a sound.

Adam and I stared in amazement. There was no doubt about it; the teacup had simply vanished! The twins were smiling smugly at us.

"Wow!" said Adam. "That's wild!"

"'Wild' is right," I echoed.

"A simple enough thing," said the twin who had done the trick. He laughed. "Edwin, why don't you demonstrate some basic telekinesis?"

"Teleka-what?" asked Adam.

"Telekinesis," said Edwin. "The ability to move objects without touching them." He set his face in a mask of concentration and stared at the other teacup. As I watched him, I noticed he had a small scar over his right eyebrow. It was the only way in which he differed from his brother. I turned my attention back to the teacup. It rose off the table about two feet and stayed there. Edwin smiled at us as the cup sank slowly back onto the tabletop.

Adam and I were very impressed. Still, we had seen so many strange and fantastic things on Phobos that we recovered our wits quickly. I apologized for doubting the power of magic.

"That's quite all right," said Peter. "Doubt is something we encounter on our visits here."

"So you *are* from someplace else," I said. "I could hear your accents. Where do you live?"

"We were born in England but now live in another land," said Edwin. Rapidly changing the subject, he added, "I would think you two to be quite brave."

Adam and I looked at each other. It was an odd statement. Adam laughed uneasily.

"Well, we've been in some tough situations," he said, "but I don't think we're any kind of heroes."

"I think you are wrong there," said Peter. The twins glanced at each other and nodded. Then they stood up and looked at Adam and me in a way that made me very nervous.

"What goes on?" I asked.

"Mentor has need of you," said Edwin.

His words puzzled me, but what happened next was far more

116

The teacup rose off the table about two feet and stayed there.

unsettling. The pizzeria seemed to vanish, and for a few seconds I felt myself spinning in a black void. I closed my eyes in terror. When I opened them, I was a long way from Sanford's Pizzeria.

Brilliant sunlight made me blink. Looking around, I saw what looked like a tropical garden. To my left was Adam, looking as confused as I felt.

The twins stood in front of us. They had transported us to some far-off place, I thought. But to what purpose?

"What's the meaning of this?" I demanded. "Where are we?"

"You will learn the answers to those and other questions shortly," said Edwin.

"I'm afraid that won't do," I said angrily. "Why have you brought us here? If it's another demonstration of your magic, it's not necessary. We already believe. Kindly take us back to Sanford's."

"Yeah," said Adam, "the lunch hour will be starting soon, and Sanford will be back."

"I'm afraid it is not possible to return you to the pizzeria at this time," Peter said. "But we will explain why you were brought here." He frowned in concentration, looking at an empty space in the grass. A moment later two polished marble benches appeared there. The twins told us to sit.

"What's going on?" asked Adam, obeying.

"You are in the Royal Gardens of King Talmar, in the city of Mentor. Mentor is located on Anphor, a world far removed from your solar system. You were brought here because you two are to save our world."

"What!" Adam and I spoke as one.

"Let us explain," continued Edwin. "Anphor is a world made up of talented individuals from other worlds. Its people are chosen because they are in some way special. It has existed for a very long time in peace and harmony, but now that harmony is threatened.

"There are two large cities on Anphor. These are Mentor and Lildor. As we have told you, you are now in the service of Mentor and . . ."

"Are we now?" I interrupted. "We have no knowledge of your world, or feeling for it. You cannot just whisk us off our home planet and tell us what to do. We're not slaves!"

"If you'll be patient," said Edwin, "it will be made clear why you were chosen. A wizard foresaw that one day a time of trouble would come to Anphor. He said that a beast and a boy would be found to save us. My brother and I have searched for these two on many worlds. And we have found them: you are the two. We sensed it from the first. At any rate, it will be impossible for you to return to Earth until your work here is finished."

His words carried a ring of finality that made me shiver. Looking at Adam I said slowly, "We will listen to what you have to say."

"Good," said Peter Cambricke. "Now for a little history. Mentor and Lildor have existed peaceably together for ages. Then, about a year ago, a sorcerer called Roxymo appeared in Lildor. He was able to put King Tymon of Lildor under a spell. Tymon declared war on Mentor. He ordered a group of men to come here and kill Kroleus, our king. They did this, using a form of sorcery over which our warlocks and wizards were powerless.

But we are not completely at Roxymo's mercy. In some ways we are immune to his enchanted spells."

"What do you mean?" queried Adam.

"Though we can be harmed by Roxymo's spells, we cannot be controlled by them as the people of Lildor are. He can send Lildorians to attack us, but he cannot make us turn against each other. Because we believe in peace we will not attack Lildor. But this Roxymo will stop at nothing until he has his way."

"Well, I'm sorry to hear that," said Adam, "but where do the Warthog and I fit in?"

"Before King Kroleus was killed, he called my brother and me to him. He foresaw that he did not have long to live. He showed us his Royal Scrolls, which contain the future history of Anphor. A page in them reads: 'The king, before leaving, will send two who are as one to Earth. There they will find a brown beast who speaks and his friend. They shall bring these two to Anphor to battle the evil that invades us . . .' "

"And you think that I am 'the brown beast'?" I asked.

"I do not think it," said Peter. "I *know* it, here." He placed his hand over his heart. "Kroleus told my brother and me to go to Earth to find you and bring you back with us. You will know how to defeat this wizard Roxymo and drive him away."

"But how?" I asked. My head was spinning with all these new facts. "Adam and I have no knowledge of magic. We have no strange powers, either."

"Ah," said Edwin, "there you are wrong. I think you will find there is much magic in you, Warthog. Think back on your life; were not some very unusual gifts given you?"

120

I thought at once of my power to speak and understand all languages. Such ability could only be called magical. I told the twins about it.

"You see," said Peter Cambricke, "that's proof right there. Within you are other doors as yet unopened. My brother and I will instruct you and Adam in the use of magic. And with the gift of magic go the gifts of self-understanding and wisdom, for magic alone will not be enough. 'The brown beast shall cast away evil with a shred of knowledge, spreading light,' say the Royal Scrolls. And you, Mr. Warthog, are that brown beast!"

10
Magic Showdown

Later that day Adam and I found ourselves sitting in a large comfortable room with walls of polished ivory. The twins had transported us to the Royal Palace of Mentor. They told us we would live there while they taught us magic.

First, however, they had led us through huge hallways with hundred-foot-high walls hung with fantastic pictures. The floor was covered with thick carpeting in a rainbow pattern. With each step we took, the colors shifted in dazzling patterns.

Men and women came and went through the palace hallways, moving with graceful ease. Many walked on the air itself, six feet or more above our heads. All of the races of earth were present, as well as others.

I say "others" because there are no words to describe some of the strange creatures we saw. There were a number of red dragonlike creatures, something that looked like a huge turtle that walked upright, and a couple of small white animals that resembled giraffes. Then there were other beings which rolled or slithered along the carpeting, changing shape and color each time you looked at them.

"As I told you," said Edwin, "the inhabitants of Anphor are from many different worlds. Don't worry, though; they are all intelligent and peaceful." This last statement was directed to Adam, who had been gawking nervously at a strange-looking cluster of floating bubbles that seemed to be having a conversation with a four-armed girl.

I realized I was now on a world where everyone was "different." Compared to some of the beings I saw, I was quite ordinary. So this was what it was like for most people in the universe! Because I now took pride in being who I was, I could at last appreciate my differentness. But here on Anphor, no one would give me a second glance! I was amused to realize that this fact bothered me a little.

After we had walked for hours, the twins had stopped us and transported us to the room in which we now found ourselves. They told us that the rest of the day was ours for rest and relaxation. Edwin pointed out a buzzer on the wall, which we were to ring if we needed anything. Then the twins vanished, saying they would call for us tomorrow.

"Our luck is running true to form, Adam," I said, laughing, when the twins had left. "It looks like we have stumbled into another adventure. And it seems to be a fantastic one!"

"If what those twins say is true," replied Adam, "and it *was* predicted that we save their world, well, I'd be a fool to kick and scream about it. All this talk about magic is pretty far out; but I wouldn't mind learning a few tricks. You know—hey, we've got company."

This last remark was prompted by the appearance of a pretty young girl with blue hair. She wore a long white dress and carried a tray filled with food and drink. Smiling at us, she set the tray down on a marble table in the middle of the room.

"Who are you?" asked Adam, his eyes wide.

The girl introduced herself as Tabalia, a servant of the Royal Palace of Mentor. Adam and I introduced ourselves in turn.

"I was told," said the girl with admiration in her voice, "that you are the two who have been brought from afar to defeat Roxymo."

"Yanked from afar is more like it," grinned Adam.

"How brave you must be!" she said.

"Maybe," said Adam, giggling sheepishly, "though we don't seem to have much choice. But, hey, that food looks good, and I'm starved. Let's eat! Will you join us, Tabalia?"

The three of us sat down to a wonderful lunch. None of the food was familiar to me, but it was all delightful. We ate hungrily and drank a delicious amber-colored liquid called *hearthan*.

From Tabalia we learned again that all the natives of Anphor had been selected to live there because of some special gift that set them apart from their fellows. It was a great honor, she said, to be asked to come to Mentor for any reason. The inhabitants all spoke each other's languages, though English was the most common tongue used. Tabalia told us she came from a world on

124

the far side of the sun. It had a name that Adam couldn't even begin to pronounce.

We talked for a long time after we finished our meal. Tabalia eventually left, promising that she would be back later with the evening meal. She also explained to us that in Mentor both men and women took turns doing the little jobs that keep things running smoothly. She was thrilled to have been chosen that week as our serving girl. Her particular talent was her voice. On a second's notice, she could compose a complicated piece of music in her mind and sing it. She demonstrated this for us, and I have never heard such wonderful music since that afternoon. Not only could she sing beautifully, but she could easily duplicate the sounds of an entire orchestra. Adam and I listened in awe and applauded enthusiastically when she was done.

"Quite a girl, that Tabalia," remarked Adam.

"Indeed," I agreed, noting the dreamy expression in his eyes.

We rested for the afternoon, tired out by all we had seen and learned. After the evening meal had come and gone, Adam and I bathed and got ready for bed. As I crawled under the covers, I wondered what tomorrow would bring.

The next morning I was awakened by the Fabulous Twins. Edwin stood grinning over me. Looking to my right, I saw Peter smiling down at Adam. I got out of bed, refreshed by my deep, dreamless sleep.

Tabalia brought us all a large breakfast. Afterward Edwin told me that my training in the art of magic was to begin immediately. He was to teach me while his brother instructed Adam. Edwin transported me to a round, white room.

That first day was spent "clearing" my mind and soul. As Edwin explained it, I needed to cast out unnecessary and negative thoughts. Then I would be free to begin to unlock my magical abilities. By midday Edwin said I was making splendid progress. He informed me that tomorrow we would spend the morning in meditation so that I would be in a relaxed state of mind to learn some basic "tricks."

In the next two weeks, I learned a lot. On the third day of my training, I astounded myself by being able to move objects at will. Soon I mastered the secret of levitation and could walk with ease on air. Once Edwin had put me in touch with my inner being, these things came easily. My spirit soared with the joy of what I was learning.

On the eighth day, Edwin showed me how to look into another's mind and see his or her life force, or soul. He warned me that this gift was never to be misused to gain personal power, and I vowed that I would respect it.

Then Edwin gave me an amulet which he called a "Talisman of the Life Force." He hung it around my neck and taught me how to use it both to cast spells and break those directed at me.

On the fifteenth day, Edwin announced that my training was at an end.

"Understand, Warthog," he said, "that you are still young in the ways of magic. But you and your friend Adam are willing and good at heart. That can count for more than skill.

"My brother and I have been in mental contact with Roxymo. He knows of your presence and has set a date for a confrontation. He is confident and treacherous, but he is also a fool, for he pays

126

no heed to the predictions of the Scrolls. He has agreed that if he is defeated, he will leave Anphor and return to his world. We have set tomorrow as the date of your showdown on the Astral Plane."

At these words I became afraid. Edwin looked at me closely.

"Remember," he said. "Fear and doubt are your enemies even more than Roxymo. The knowledge that your cause is good and just should be foremost in your mind. Now I will leave so you may prepare for tomorrow."

With those words, Edwin vanished. I transported myself back to the room where Adam and I slept. A few minutes later Adam came in.

"Tomorrow's the day, Wart," he said. "Roxymo, watch out!"

"Yes," I said. "Let's call for Tabalia and get some food. Then I think we should spend some time in meditation, for we have a difficult task ahead of us."

The following morning we awoke early and ate breakfast with Tabalia. She cried when the twins came for us. Adam took her by the hand and kissed her fingertips. She blushed, and returned his kiss upon his right cheek. Before she left she kissed me on the same spot.

"May the Higher Power which governs good in the universe go with you today," were her last words before she vanished.

"We have just spoken with Roxymo," said Edwin. "His spirit awaits you on the lower realms of the Astral Plane. We will guide you there."

Without another word Edwin reached out his right hand and placed it on my forehead. I saw Peter do the same to Adam.

A moment later I felt my body melt away as my spirit left it. My life force sped upward, led by Edwin Cambricke, magician of Mentor.

During my days of training, Edwin had told me what to expect on the Astral Plane. Still, I was not prepared for the strangeness of the place. Pitch blackness changed into bright white light. Heat alternated with cold. I tried to keep myself calm.

"That's it," I heard Edwin's voice in my mind. "Do not be fooled by the contrasts here. In a moment things will settle down."

In a moment they did. I found myself floating in the center of a huge gray valley. Steam rose from the rocks below and around me. Edwin had told me that the lower realms of the Astral Plane were ruled by evil and the higher realms by good. We would be battling an evil foe on his own ground, for Roxymo would not fight us anywhere else.

I felt Adam's spirit floating next to mine. Together, we reached out with our minds to search for Roxymo's spirit. I sensed a surge of power from a spot to my left. Looking down, I saw a figure standing on a cliff below us. Circling him were a number of batlike creatures. I called Adam's attention to him.

"It must be Roxymo!" thought Adam. I could hear all his thoughts in my mind.

Adam flung a mental bolt of thunder at the evil wizard. The figure vanished, laughing wickedly.

"A trick!" I told Adam. "That figure was an illusion." Then, from above us, I heard a voice. Over our heads I saw the ghostly shape of a huge, grinning head. My instincts told me this face was Roxymo. As I studied it, the features shifted and changed.

128

Waves of greed and wickedness spread from the head and seemed to swirl around my body.

"The brown beast comes," Roxymo called. "Oh, I tremble!"

"You are on your own now," Edwin's voice said. I felt his spirit leaving me.

So it was that Adam and I found ourselves face to face with the sinister Roxymo. Looking at the grinning head, I shuddered.

"I will give you one chance to surrender," I heard the wizard's voice say in my head. "Do this, and you will be spared great pain and suffering. I can cast a spell that will scatter your life forces to the far reaches of the universe. It will be as if you had never existed at all. What do you say?"

"No, Roxymo," I thought at him. "We will battle you until one or both of us should fall!"

The great face darkened. "Very well," it said. "So you wish to do battle. It bores me, this game of casting spells back and forth. But I will play until you weaken. Then, I'll hurl both your souls into the Void of Fear, where you will drift in terror and pain for eternity!"

With a blood-curdling laugh, he sent a spell at me. If I had not been trained by Edwin Cambricke, I would never have known what hit me. But being schooled in sorcery I felt and saw the cloudy black mist approaching. As it wrapped itself around my astral body (which is another word for spirit), I felt myself pulled in a dozen directions. Panic welled in my chest. One part of my mind saw the faces of Horgor and the young warthogs who used to tease and hurt me. They were laughing and chanting "Die, die!" With each chant I felt weaker and more afraid.

Remembering Edwin's warning about fear and doubt, I fought down these emotions. I thought instead of good things: how I had grown to respect myself; of my love for my parents and for Adam and Troy. The faces vanished, slowly, as my confidence returned. I realized that Roxymo had reached into my memory to pull out my worst fears. Feeling myself growing stronger, I called upon the forces of reason to throw the spell back on Roxymo. The mist rolled away from me toward his huge floating face.

It seemed to go into his eyes. But when the mist had vanished, somehow the face was more solid and powerful than before.

I sensed that Roxymo had used the same spell on Adam. I communicated to my friend how to combat it. My mental message succeeded, for a moment later Adam had hurled his own black mist of horror back at the wizard.

I watched again as the eyes seemed to eat up the evil spell, and the face to grow stronger. I thought, with a start, it was as though Roxymo ate evil.

Though time has no meaning on the Astral Plane, it seemed like hours that Adam and I did battle with Roxymo. He sent spells as quickly as we could defend ourselves. I did not again make the mistake of hurling a spell back at him. I told Adam not to either, for our spells only increased Roxymo's power. The only thing we could do was to destroy his spells, which we did by erecting a mental shield that absorbed them. This took up a lot of energy, and I began to tire. I could feel my reflexes becoming slower. Roxymo, for his part, seemed to have an endless supply of energy.

130

The first faint stirrings of despair had begun to creep into my heart. As I pushed these feelings away, an idea began to take form in my brain. I guarded it carefully so Roxymo would not read my thought.

"Roxymo!" I called out mentally. "We cannot keep up this battle much longer. We see that your power is too great. Perhaps we can make a deal! Only please, do not destroy us!"

"Ha!" Harsh laughter echoed in my brain. "You plead with me for mercy in an astral duel! Only one shall emerge victorious today. That one shall be Roxymo! But I will destroy you as painlessly as possible if you say that you give in."

"Don't do it!" Adam's voice pulsed in my head.

Surrender was not on my mind, however. While Roxymo spoke I had been mentally probing his soul. It was ugly and terrible to look upon, but I held it in my mind's eye. Then, exerting all my will, I called up knowledge of the goodness within me, giving it shape and power.

I thought how in my life good had always beaten evil. I thought of bees and Torks. I thought of evil dictators and greedy poachers. I thought of jewel thieves.

I thought how in all my dealings with the forces of evil, I had won because I cared about the people I helped. With each thought, I felt my power grow stronger.

When it had reached its peak, I muttered a spell into my Talisman of the Life Force: "Powers that be, take the knowledge of my heart; send Roxymo this spell, and let love tear him apart!"

A multicolored mist sprang from my astral body. It entered Roxymo's eyes. Instantly, the face began to break apart. At the same time I heard the tortured screams of the wizard ringing in my mind. I felt the forces of good and evil doing battle within him, shattering the blackness of his soul. I heard Adam cheering mentally. Then I felt myself falling backwards into space.

After what seemed years, I awoke (I was later informed that it was only the next day). I was in my bed in the room Adam and I had shared on Anphor. Sitting around the bed were Edwin and Peter Cambricke, Adam Armstrong, and Tabalia. I smiled weakly at them.

"Wart's all right!" shouted Adam. "He's awake!"

"Yes," said Edwin Cambricke proudly. "Congratulations, Warthog! You have destroyed the menace of Roxymo and made Anphor safe again. His spell over the people of Lildor has been broken! How do you feel?"

"Not too bad," I said. "How are you feeling, Adam?"

"Oh, I'll survive," said my friend happily. "You did most of the work, you know, Wart. All I did was destroy spells, but you came up with the winning one. How'd you do it?"

"I—I just used what I know, I guess," I said.

Edwin cleared his throat. "You know," he began, "you accomplished what all the knowledge and magic in Mentor could not. My brother and I thank you for all the people of Anphor. We'd like you to consider staying here and becoming our king. That is, eventually. You still have a bit more to learn! But it is also written in our Royal Scrolls that 'a brown beast shall one day lead Mentor.' "

I looked from one twin to the other in disbelief. Then I looked at Adam, who was gazing tenderly at me.

132

"Go ahead, Wart," he said. "You can't go on turning down these offers forever, you know."

My head felt light and I was thirsty. As though he had read my thoughts, Peter Cambricke handed me a bowl of *hearthan*. I lapped up about half of it. It made me feel much better.

"Well," I said, at length. "I think I'll at least consider your offer."

Everyone looked pleased, and I felt a warm glow spreading inside my chest.

"Yes," I spoke again. "I will consider it. And if I can consider that, I might just think about taking a name for myself, too."

"Hey," said Adam, whistling.

"Hold on there, Adam," I chuckled. "I said *might*. I know one thing for sure: the kingship of this world would mean very little to me if you and Troy stayed on Earth. You fellows mean more to me than I can say. But if I did stay, it would be because I want to, not because I'm afraid to go back among humans and other animals."

I closed my eyes, feeling drowsy. An image of Old Zareemba came into my mind. I remembered his words of almost a year ago. He'd told me that one day I would appreciate my differentness. I knew now that no other warthog could have done the things I'd done. I accepted myself as I was, and I was glad to be me.

As I drifted off to sleep, I smiled to myself. And I knew without a doubt that back in the bush, Old Zareemba smiled, too.

Epilogue

Outside the window of the Warthog's study, the night was nearly pitch black. Inside the study, the Warthog glanced toward the grandfather clock in the corner of the room. He noted that it read 2:00 A.M.

Her bright eyes open and alert, Irene Springer sat on the edge of her chair. "Do go on, Mr. Warthog," she said. "I am not sleepy at all, and I am anxious to learn what occurred next. Was peace restored to Anphor? What did you and Adam do next? And what happened to Troy? I can see from your place in your *Tales*, which you have consulted from time to time, that there is a great deal more to tell. It is incredible that at so young an age, you were exposed to so much adventure!"

The Warthog laughed, and the laugh turned into a yawn, which he made a valiant effort to suppress. "Irene," he said, "though the hearing of my life story may keep you awake, I fear that the telling of it has rather knocked me out. I find that as I grow older, my need for a good night's rest becomes stronger. Tomorrow evening I would be more than pleased to continue my reminiscences, but for tonight, at least, I fear my story is at an end."